Murry's Malady

Malady

A Story of Murder for Profit

Alistair Newton

ISBN 10: 0-9788424-0-5
ISBN 13: 978-0-9788424-0-6

Printed in the United States of America

PROLOGUE

*"Killin' a man wid a gun is a terrible thing,
but there's worse, like tellin' him you love him
just before you kill him." Willie Monk.*

I never met Murry Berman but I liked him. We had nothing in common. He was a corporate attorney who left his home and family on Long Island every morning and fought the traffic into New York City. I'm an independent insurance investigator. I go to work occasionally, only when I have to. I had to do a lot of digging to find out what happened that morning but I think I finally have it right. This is the way it was.

Before Murry left his home that morning, Liddy handed him a list of things to do for the day. Then she gave him his briefcase and a plastic coffee travel mug. He kissed his kids goodbye and went out to his car. As he backed out of the driveway, he glanced at Liddy standing on the small front porch, waving goodbye. She wore tight, faded jeans, no shoes, an East Harbour Little League T-shirt with no bra. Murry thought to himself, "Nice body." She was still a good-looking woman even after three children and all those years of working while Murry went nights to N.Y.U. He thought about how he finally earned his law degree and they fulfilled their dream of moving "out on the Island". Now they had it made: at least in Murry's mind they had it made, "If only Lydia would settle down and enjoy it." He thought of last night and the brutal argument they had about him being more active in local town affairs. He tried to put it out of his mind as he made the turn onto Shore Drive and headed his six-year-old BMW towards town. Lydia was always pushing for something bigger and better. She was never satisfied. So, Murry worked hard, spent his money wisely and hoped for the best. What else could a man do? With Liddy, you could never win.

Shore Drive made a sharp turn around the coastline of Little Peconic Bay and Murry suddenly realized he did not have his seat belt fastened. Reaching behind with his left hand, he grasped the belt and gave it a firm pull. "STUCK!" He pulled again. Still stuck, so he gave it several sharp jerks. "Damn!" It was really jammed. "It's going to be one of those days," he muttered to the windshield. He slowed, made a sharp left onto Cross Street to avoid the center of town and headed for the Long Island Expressway Link. Other cars joined him in a steady line and so began the daily grind of driving into the city. Just before the interchange that led to the L.I.E., Murry turned off into a small shopping center and pulled up to the drive-in window of a Coffee'N Dunk.

Murry liked the Coffee'N Dunk chain because for every ten cups of coffee you got one free. With a smile, he handed the plastic travel mug to the girl at the window and said, "Good Morning". Wendy, a summer employee, returned the greeting, took the cup and popped the lid. It was the same every morning. This little man with thick horn rimmed glasses came in and bought coffee with cream and two sugars, stirred. The other girls thought he was funny looking but Wendy told them, "I think he's sort of cute, and besides he's always very nice and lets me keep the change." This morning it took her a little longer than usual, for some reason, and when Wendy handed Murry the full cup, its lid tightly secured, she gave him a strange look and giggled. He was struggling with the jammed seat belt and did not notice the giggles or strange looks as he drove away.

His mind was now focused on the road and the trip into New

York City. This was his time to think, plan, and get geared up for the workday ahead. There was no talk radio, news or music, just concentrate on getting the mental juices going. A board meeting was scheduled in the afternoon and Murry began to tick off the items for which he would be responsible. There was one point, about which, he would have to be especially careful. His boss, Arnold Kilmer, wanted to buy out a Delaware shell corporation and absorb a number of smaller high tech companies through some complicated stock swaps. "Then the stupid bastard will want to transfer everything off shore and try to hide the assets to avoid taxes," he muttered to himself. "The IRS is already onto that sort of deal so forget it, Arnold," he said as if Arnold were sitting next to him in the car.

On the L.I.E. he sipped his coffee while he played the usual game of "dodge and dive." A kid in an old brown Ford kept cutting him off until Murry decided it wasn't worth the hassle and let him go ahead. Now he started to relax and get into it as the traffic moved along. His coffee was almost gone except for a little in the bottom of the cup, which he did not seem able to finish. Something was plugging the hole in the lid so he pried it off and looked inside. What he saw made him want to throw up. He felt a growing tightness in his throat and his stomach began to heave. He tried to loosen his collar but he couldn't reach it. He wanted to stop but couldn't find the brake. Everything was spinning and far away. His last thoughts probably were, "Why? Why me?"

The police said he must have been going over seventy when he hit the ditch. Had he been wearing his seat belt, they thought he might have survived. "He lost control. It was a tragedy. He will be missed," said the newspaper article.

Like I said, I never met Murry Berman but the more I learn about him, the more I like him. He had a lot of courage. That's something I can respect in a man. ❄

CHAPTER ONE

The wind was steady, increasing from the southwest but the waves were becoming confused as the larger swells of the open Atlantic collided with the short chop of Long Island Sound. The yawl took a wave head-on and I got a face full of spray, reminding me that sailing is not a spectator sport. I corrected about fifteen degrees to port and let out a few feet on the main sheet for an easier ride.

The Gentle Spirit dipped her bow and rode smoothly over the next wave. I didn't have to touch the wheel to hold course. Off the port bow I spotted two fins. Dolphins? I saw several sets of the familiar little triangles, breaking the surface, as I got closer. Mako sharks, maybe a dozen, swimming in a pack. Wouldn't be many other fish in the area with these fellows around. "Hunter Packs," I said to the wind. I applied pressure to the wheel to avoid the sharks and came back on course, my bow pointing just to the south of Orient Point with Plum Island on my left.

I was headed home after a lazy day of sailing. Timing was everything and I thought I had it figured. Leaving on an outgoing tide in the morning, I made good time south of Gardiners Island and out into the Atlantic. The channel south of Gardiners is tricky and I always like to try it at high tide when I'm fresh. From there I made for Great Gull Island to the north, where I tied up to the pilings on the lee side of the island for lunch and a short break, then back again on an incoming tide. A low misty fog was rolling in from the north.

I saw the New London ferry headed for Orient Point. It had been a boring day, all things considered. I luffed until the ferry pulled abreast and then hauled the main sheet tight, set the jib hard-by and stood the Gentle Spirit on her head. The difference in speed between the ferry and my craft disappeared as she took the bit of the wind in her teeth and plunged ahead, showing herself to be the thoroughbred she was built to be. The ferry captain would slow his speed as he approached the channel of the gut and that was when the fun would begin.

The ferry's rails were suddenly lined with passengers pointing to us, waving and cheering us on as we raced the bigger boat. I cut inside the bell entering Plum Gut and took a bearing on the marker on Midway Shoal leaving the main channel open to the larger boat. The ferry slowed and the Gentle Spirit showed her stuff more then ever as we pulled ahead. I waved goodbye to the passengers at the rails of the ferry and received a standing ovation as it turned into the landing docks at Orient Point. Like I said, it was a slow day.

The trip past Shelter Island to Greenport was uneventful. A welcoming committee waited for me on the main dock at Green's Marine. "Boy, Mr. O'Keefe, you came in just at the right time," said a tall, lanky, blond seventeen year old.

"Why's that, Timmy?"

"There's a man on the telephone, says he has to talk to you. Says it's an emergency. He's been calling all day. I told him I saw your sails up the channel so he said he would hold. He's still up there waiting on the phone. Want me to take care of the boat, Mr. O'Keefe?"

"Just make sure she's secure. I'll settle up with you later. Oh, and would you set up the battery charger and fill the water tanks. I want her ready to go." I walked up to the main office and answered the phone.

"Bill? Bill? Is that really you? Man, I've been trying to get you all day. Don't you ever check in?"

"I'm on vacation, Harry. I don't check in when I'm on vacation. I go sailing and there's no telephone on my boat. I don't like to talk to people when I'm on vacation."

"Don't try to kid me. You don't take vacations. You just call it that because you're not working."

"I'm still in business but I choose to go sailing instead of sitting at a desk like all you other slugs so this better be good. What do you want, Harry?"

"You can't believe it. It's the worse mess I've ever seen. This claim got buried in someone's file until this morning, Friday morning, so now we can't do anything on it until Monday. No, make that Tuesday because Monday is a holiday, Labor Day. Can you believe it? It's Labor Day weekend and I get this thing handed to me..."

"Hold it right there, Harry. You know how I feel about State Mutual. I swore I would never work for you people again."

"It's all right. I called John Stanley in Omaha and he said to do whatever it took to straighten it out. I mentioned you. He's president of the company now so that's about as high as you can go..."

"I don't trust John Stanley and he doesn't like me. I get 10% when I work, which I doubt you people will pay, so this conversation is academic."

"John Stanley said we would pay. Believe me, it's alright, you'll get paid. You're my last hope. If this thing goes through, I'll lose my job. Bill, for old times sake, please just listen."

"O.K., but no promises. No one will work for you again if you stiff me. I'll personally see to it. You hear me?"

"Yes, you bet. Here it is. Deceased is Murry Berman: male, thirty-five years of age, corporate attorney, residence 1315 Bay Circle, East Harbour. Survived by wife-beneficiary Lydia, thirty-one, Stephan age 9, David age 7, Susan age 5. Cause of death, auto accident on the way to work. Policy written June 10th for three million, straight twenty-year term life. Physical completed June 26th. The policy issued July 16th, death occurred August 1st, four weeks ago and the claim got buried, like I said, until this morning."

"So, what's the problem? You called me about this because someone got greedy and wrote a three-mil policy? Get real, Harry, you don't need me. You got an internal problem. Solve it and send me a Christmas card"

"Wait...Bill, wait. Don't hang up. It gets worse."

"What could be worse?"

"You'll never believe it. How this application made it through Underwriting and into the files without someone stopping it is a pure miracle of corporate negligence. Worst part is if death occurred accidentally, the policy pays double indemnity. That's $6 million." He paused for effect. "Bill? Bill? Are you still there?"

I could hardly talk. "Yeh...I'm here." I was stunned at the enormity of it all. "You mean that nobody caught this before now?"

"That's right and if I don't stop it, I'm out of a job."

"And if I straighten this out you say John Stanley has agreed to pay me my usual fee of ten percent. That's $600,000."

"That's right, and it's guaranteed. I have John Stanley's word on it."

"Okay, but remember, I get 10%, right?"

"You're an angel. I'll get a messenger to you by tomorrow so you can be on the case by Monday morning."

"No, listen up! I'll contact you in a couple of hours. Stand by your fax machine with everything you've got on this case and start an internal investigation. I want backgrounds on everyone who's connected: the agent, policy holder, relatives of everyone, the town, the physician, the underwriting staff including secretaries and mail boys, janitors, anyone who had access to that policy."

"You have to be kidding. That'll take all night. What'll I tell my staff? They don't know about this."

"Somebody on your staff knows a lot about it or it never would have happened. Tell them you're running a trial audit and offer triple overtime. After all, Harry, have you got anything else going on in your life right now?"

"Ah … no, I guess not."

It was no longer a slow day. ※

CHAPTER TWO

East Harbour was a step beyond the typical resort town. With a growing year-round population, it could be classified as a commuter's bedroom community. Its location on Little Peconic Bay made it more attractive to the big city commuter and helped drive up real estate values. I was going in blind. Had I known what I was getting into, I would have turned around and headed back to my sailboat, but such are the Fates.

The picturesque town square was surrounded by old restored colonial and federalist homes, a white church with a tall spire, the town hall, a police station and a firehouse. I parked my Caddy in a paved lot between the town hall and police station.

My first stop was the town clerk's office. It was late on a Friday afternoon, Labor Day weekend, but it was open. Doors with smoked glass windows opened off a long hall down the middle of the building with wide board flooring that creaked when I walked. I picked the window that said Town Clerk and banged on the wood-work next to it. There was more creaking of floorboards and the rustle of feet on carpet. Then a window to my right opened, revealing a small balding man in his late sixties, half-specs hanging on his nose, cotton shirt open at the top, and a bland smile on his face. He had the look of wisdom and I knew there was probably no way I'd fool this old duck.

"Hi, there!" I stuck out my hand but he didn't take it. "I'm interested in a piece of property here in town and I took the chance someone would be in. My lucky day, you're here."

"We have a lot of property." He smiled." Any particular one or you just shopping around?"

"I'm interested in one particular piece but I'm trying to be discreet." I tried acting unsure of myself.

"Well, why don't you just give me a hint, like the name and location of the property and its present owner for starters?" He'd played this game before.

"I'm looking at a place on Bay Circle. The Berman place."

"You fellows don't waste much time." His smile was gone. "What is it you want to know about the Berman's?"

"Plot plan, tax liens, permits, variances, probate...whatever you can give me."

"Stay right there." He disappeared, shutting the window behind him. He returned in less than a minute and produced a manila file marked BERMAN. "No liens, no variances, no probate yet, taxes are up to date." He was leafing through the file. There's a copy of the plot plan. Berman's is #235, right there," he pointed to a lot of minimal size in the middle of a very large development marked Cirelli Construction.

Murry Berman lived in a three bedroom raised ranch, tax-assessed at $695,000 in the middle of a development of raised ranches. He was a lawyer with three kids and his taxes were paid. I looked at the little man with the specs and decided to try the friendly approach.

"Do you have any ideas I might find helpful about this?"

"Like what in general, young fellow? You trying to pick Mr. Berman's bones or is it his wife you're interested in?" He didn't buy the friendly approach.

"I'm trying to be Murry's friend. I sort of owe him one."

"More likely, you're from some insurance company and you're trying to get out of paying his widow the money you owe her."

"Could be, or maybe I'm trying to locate her so I can give her more than she deserves."

"Yeh, sure." He laughed. "You're all alike! Just doing your job, right. Pick the poor widow's bones as soon as the husband is in the ground."

"You're a pretty sharp judge of character for a town clerk. I'm William O'Keefe, Bill to my friends. I am an insurance investigator and Murry Berman is my case. I was on a sailing vacation when they called me, so I'm starting out cold and I'm not sure where to begin." I put my hand out and this time he took it.

"I guess we were both masquerading some. I'm not the town clerk here. I'm the Mayor of East Harbour. Name's Calvin Kinderhook , retired from teaching up state. Came out here twelve years ago to get away. Should've kept going. It's getting more crowded here than ever. Don't feel sorry for Liddy Berman. She's the kind of woman who will land on her feet every time, and the loss of a husband won't slow her down one bit. Around here, a good yuppie housewife has all her escape routes lined up just in case, and Liddy's no exception. I knew Murry Berman, probably better than most. He was a decent sort of man. Kind of laid back and wimpy but he was all right, you know, a nice guy. I guess I'm out of line telling you all this but someone else will anyway. I just feel sorry for the kids. Around here, kids get run over and pushed aside in the stampede for success. Makes you sick to watch it." He shook his head in disgust.

"Sounds as though you liked Murry Berman."

"Well, let me put it this way, son. If I was to vote for someone in this town to die, Murry Berman wouldn't be on the list."

"You mean they vote on who's going to die in East Harbour?"

"Sometimes I wonder but you might not want to talk about it. I'd just as soon not end up on the list if there is one."

"But you're the Mayor. No one would want you dead...would they?"

"Well, probably not. You know, normally, a small town like this would just have the town council with three selectmen, but things got so complicated they agreed to change the charter. I have administrative experience so I got elected even though I'm a newcomer. You're lucky you ran into me instead of some of the locals. They aren't very friendly to outsiders. That's one reason I liked Murry. He got along fine with everyone. I'm not saying everyone liked him but he got along, and I'm going to miss him because when it came to town government, he knew his beans."

"So you're saying Murry Berman wasn't exactly well liked but he wasn't not well liked either."

"It wasn't all personality. He was chairman of the town finance committee and people seemed to accept him because he knew what to do. He was competent. If it wasn't for the way Liddy pushed him, he might have been more popular. Then there was the spider web thing." He finished up by rolling his eyes in a "you know what I mean" expression.

"The what?"

"The spider web episode." He pointed to the ceiling. "It happened right across the hall in that room over there." He pointed to a door behind me. "Follow me and I'll show you." He shut the window, went across the hall and through a door marked "Meeting Room". I followed and found myself in an old-fashioned town meeting room filled with chairs, a raised platform in the front with a long table surrounded by chairs. The ceiling was high, the floor made of old wide pine boards, and the windows were large, almost floor to ceiling, designed to let in the maximum light. Calvin went on just like he was giving a guided tour to a group of newcomers, or more like a civics lesson to some high school students.

"Now, you have to get this straight in your mind. Murry was chairing the annual budget meeting of the finance committee. That's a real important meeting because all the annual budget requests come to the finance committee where they are put together for presentation at the annual town meeting, which is supposed to happen maybe the next night or so. It's like a preliminary approval process. Problem is, the annual budget must be presented and voted on before any more bills can be paid. The finance committee can disapprove of line-item requests that aren't allowed under the by-laws. It can get real complicated, but the bottom line is that the annual budget has to be presented to the town meeting by the chairman of the finance committee, and it has to be voted on and passed before any bills can be paid." He pulled up his threadbare blue slacks and tightened the belt.

"So, what happened?" I looked around at the dark ceilings.

"When Murry went crazy, it really messed things up. The budget didn't get compiled and there was no town meeting."

"You say he went crazy?"

"Well, not really crazy. He just became sort of incapacitated and that made the whole situation crazy. We were all sitting up there on the platform around that table. This used to be our meeting room before the town got too big. Now we hold our town meetings over at the high school gym. This room is for smaller groups like the finance committee that night last January. The night they met, everyone was up here at the head table." He walked to the platform and placed his hands on the table as if trying to contact a spirit at a séance.

"Murry was sitting in the middle chair with his back to the wall and I was over there at the other end of the table near the windows. Everyone else was sitting around in the chairs just like you see them right now...the chairs, I mean, like you see the chairs right now." I think maybe Calvin was seeing the faces of the people as they were that night.

"I understand. So, what happened next that was so crazy?"

"Yeh, well!" He shook himself as if coming back from some place far away. "Everything seemed alright at first. We were at it about a half hour and it looked like we might be doing it right for a change. You know, these things work sometimes and then they don't, and it takes longer if they don't. Murry, now, he seemed to know how to handle it, and when someone would interrupt or get out of hand, he would just settle them right down, put them back in their place and move on to the next item. I was really impressed. We came to the new sewer project, which is a real big item, and Sophie Gates, the police chief's wife, pipes up about a spider web up there in the corner." He pointed up behind the table to the corner over the windows. "Why, hell, I couldn't even see the damn thing at first, it was so dark up there, but Sophie, she could see lint on the moon on a dark rainy night." He stopped, shook his head and looked at the floor. "Well, we all knew Murry didn't like spiders and stuff like that. Why, nobody likes spiders, and besides, this meeting was damned important, so everyone was trying to be on their best behavior, but not Sophie Gates. She couldn't keep her mouth shut if her life hung in the balance and silence was the only cure. 'Look at that', she yelled, right in the middle of the sewer project, line item #2. I'll remember that to my dying day. Why couldn't she have just shut her big fat mouth?" He looked at the floor and shook his head again.

"Well, she wouldn't let it go. She just kept yippin' and pointin' up there at that spider web until she had the whole meeting adjourned. Somebody went for a dust mop and a broom, someone else came up with a ladder, Sophie donated her own personal can of Get-Dust which she just happened to have in her car, and man, I wanna tell yah, we destroyed that spider web and any creepy-crawly things within the general radius of this end of the meeting room. Then... if that wasn't enough, Sophie, she started in about the bats and all the rats and mice and there might even be snakes and we oughta put something on the budget about bombing the town hall. You know what I mean by bombing, don't you? Chemical warfare against nature and humans alike...bomb it all and whatever lives must belong here afterwards."

"What was Murry doing all this time?"

"Well, I noticed Murry didn't move from his chair the whole time. He just smiled and acted like it was all a big joke, kept flipping papers and reading like the meeting was still called to order and everyone was still paying attention. Then, I didn't really pay attention to him when the ladder arrived and the real business of killing that spider web got underway. Everyone seemed to get in on the act, and when Sophie proceeded to spray Get-Dust all over the place it was sorta every man, woman, child and insect for themselves. She went at it like she was out to get every germ and destroy every dust ball in the world. Man, you shoulda been there. That's when I stepped back and noticed Murry Berman was in trouble."

"Is that when he got crazy?"

"No, not crazy, just in trouble. He'd slipped down in his chair like he was going underneath the table for a look at something, feet first. His hands were up at his throat, clawing at his collar, trying to rip it open. He was white...real white...like a ghost, and having trouble breathing, gasping for breath, drooling from the mouth. Man, I don't ever want to see something like that again. His eyes were all bugged out and rolling around and he started frothing at the mouth, you know, dribbling sort of down the chin."

"So what happened then, Cal?"

"I called the ambulance and we got him up to County Hospital. What a mess. We couldn't finish the budget meeting until a new chairman pro-tem was appointed. That took a special meeting of the town council, and two of the three selectmen were fishing and not due back till the next day just before noontime, so we had to postpone the annual town meeting for almost a month due to conflicting schedules. What a mess. We couldn't pay our bills, town employees went without, road repairs were halted, the sewer project got backed up, excuse the pun. The school budget kept operating because it was on a separate warrant...What a mess, and all because Murry Berman didn't like spiders."

"Not exactly, Calvin. Not exactly."

"What do you mean?" The room was growing darker. Calvin looked older in the growing shadows of the evening.

"It's the fear of long legged, creepy, crawly, bug-like creatures that have a multitude of legs and build webs to catch their prey which they usually kill by sucking their vital juices a little at a time."

"You seem to know a lot about this sort of thing."

"I've seen it before." I was thinking of the jungle and Viet Nam.

"Sounds a lot like Liddy Berman, if you ask me."

I left Mayor Calvin Kinderhook looking at his canvas boat shoes, shaking his head in disbelief at the way life could bite back. ✺

CHAPTER THREE

I walked around the corner to the parking lot and found a policeman standing next to my Caddy writing a parking ticket. He was big around with a bull neck and a pinhead. A red face supported a small cap with gold braids on the visor. He carried a Smith and Wesson .357 Magnum on his hip, a real man's shooting iron. His nametag read 'Myron Gates-Chief' and he registered a mean scowl when I approached."

"Hello Officer." I imitated a friendly citizen but he ignored me

"Did I do something wrong?" He finished writing, tore the ticket from his book and handed it to me.

"Fifty dollars! You got to be kidding!"

"We don't kid about these things, buddy! You're parked in a restricted area, reserved for town business only. You shoulda know'd better."

"Look here, ahh, Chief, I'm sorry if I parked where I shouldn't have, but there's no sign saying this is a restricted area, so how was I to know?"

"I'm gonna do you a favor," he sneered. "Usually, I don't bother to explain the obvious to you big city cats because you're too smart to understand us little country people and our strange ways. Just be glad I'm in a good mood or you'd have yourself a ride to the office and a chance to try our holding cell for your smart mouth. Everybody knows these parking spaces are reserved for town residents doin' town business at the town hall and since I don't recognize you or your car, I know right away you're not a town resident. Now, since the town hall is closed and has been since 3:00 o'clock, I know you're not on town business and you're parked in a restricted area." He paused to catch his breath, his face growing redder. "So you get to pay a fifty dollar fine...Have a nice day!" He turned and proceeded to walk across the parking lot to the police station. I waited until I had my car door open and he was about twenty yards away.

"Hey, Chief!"

"What?" He spun around, his hand on his shooting iron.

"You're absolutely right. You're logic goes to the veritable outer limits of my credible comprehension, and I should be fined for my gross ignorance and stupidity, so same to you, buddy...Have a nice one yourself!" I slammed the car door, started the engine, shifted into reverse and floored it, barely missing Chief Myron Gates, who was still standing there, red faced and gasping for breath in the middle of the parking lot, contemplating my words of wisdom. As I shot out of the parking lot, I waved just to make sure he knew I was still friendly.

Never hurts to keep on the good side of the local police, and as my dear old grandmother used to say, "A smile is never wasted". She never met the police chief of East Harbour.

One thing for sure, I was off on the wrong foot with the local police. Calvin said the locals weren't friendly, but Myron Gates went beyond that. He was just plain bulldog mean. Sophie Gates was behind the spider web thing. Coincidence? Maybe!...Ahh, what a tangled web we weave.

The original town consisted of colonial homes built when wealth was counted by the size of your house. This extended about a half mile down to the harbor, opening out into Great Peconic Bay. I followed the shoreline and found a Daylight Inn. The sun was low in the western sky and I was hungry.

I stopped the Caddy about twenty yards from the front door. It was a typical modern cement block building, four stories high with a flat roof and sliding glass doors opening out onto individual porches overlooking the asphalt parking lot. Small, untrimmed shrubs about 5' high, flanked the double glass front doors, and extended along the front of the building. The grass around the shrubs and pavement needed cutting. Broken glass, aluminum cans and papers decorated the whole scene. I took my bag and went into the lobby. A girl in her teens behind the counter managed to enter my credit card number into the hotel computer after several tries and handed me a key to room #210. Her nametag read Shelly C. and she never smiled or said thank you.

"Back of the building. Can't expect much. No reservation on a Labor Day weekend. Will you be staying long?"

"Not long, Shelly. I'd hate to tie up a nice room like that in such a busy place on a holiday weekend." I smiled and took the stairway off the back of the lobby instead of the elevator. Never hurts to explore. The room was at the back of the building, overlooking another parking lot and the town beyond. No ocean, no porch, cheaper rate. The suckers at the front of the building paid more. I placed a call to Harry Dondi and got his secretary, Peggy Hughes.

"Hi, babe. Where's Harry?"

"Harry's hitting the head, handsome. When are you coming into the city to see me?"

"My heart's burning with desire for you, Peg, my girl. If only it would rain so I can't go sailing, I'd come and take you out for lunch, dinner and breakfast in bed."

"I'll be waiting anxiously the next time I see a rain cloud, O'Keefe, you liar. Now, what do you want that doesn't involve sex?"

"Ah, Peggy, my love, you turn me on when you talk mean to me. Here I am, sitting in a green hotel room, number 210, in East Harbour, Daylight Inn, fax number," I read it off the telephone card on the night stand, "and all you can do is taunt me with rejection when you should be considering how a single investigator should spend a long, lonely weekend in a strange town with no one to help him pass the time."

"If I know you, William, and I believe I do, you'll find some entertainment before the night is out and you'll forget all about me.

So, I'll send the file we've got on this Murry Berman thing as soon as you hang up the telephone and let me get to work, and I'd advise you to get right over to that fax machine and grab this stuff because Harry doesn't want anyone but you to see it. Also, Harry's working on that other stuff. The whole office is digging around in the archives and back rooms trying to scare up what you want. I sure as hell hope this isn't another one of your wild goose chases, because everyone is going to be mad as you know what if we're just wasting our time."

"This is not a drill. We're talking big money, $6 million worth. Pretty important wild goose chase, Huh?" I could hear Peg catch her breath. Harry hadn't told her. "Love you as always, Peg. Goodbye." She said the same. I took a quick shower and went downstairs. Shelly C. was standing behind the desk, staring bewildered at the fax machine.

"Ahh...you have my messages coming in on your machine. Just tear them off and hand them to me as they come out, Shelly." She gave me a frown.

"I don't know about this. I've never had to handle one of these things before. Maybe it would be better if you came back in the morning. The daytime manager is on and he can help you."

"That won't work, Shelly. This may be a holiday weekend for other people but I need those files now to do my work. Why don't you just give them to me and we'll settle up in the morning. How's that sound?"

"This never happened to me before. I don't know if I should let you just use our fax machine like this. Mr. Wallace, he sort of owns this hotel, he wouldn't like it if I did something I shouldn't without asking first. I need this job or I can't go back to school this fall. I'd be stuck in this lousy town another winter." Her eyes started to water.

"Can you call Mr. Wallace and maybe ask him for me if you can just sort of reach out your little old hand and tear off the paper from the fax machine and hand it to me?" I was starting to lose it.

"Oh, no! I can't do that. He left strict instructions not to be disturbed. If I call, he'll know I messed up and, boy, you don't know him when he gets mad. Wow, is he scary! You'll have to wait until tomorrow. I'm sorry but you're not worth losing this job over." She had made up her mind. That's all I needed. I ceased being friendly.

"Well, I'll tell you what, Shelly! How about I call him for you and tell him that maybe you really don't know what's going on and let him take it from there?" The look on her face told me I'd struck home.

"I've got another idea." She picked up the telephone and punched two buttons. "Miss Wilson, to the front desk, please." She hung up, looked me straight in the eye with a "you'll see" expression and we both waited. In less than a minute a woman came around the corner to the left of the front desk. A sign on the wall pointed the direction from which she'd come. It read "OFFICES". She was about thirty, 5'6", auburn hair, bluish-green eyes, slim but strong build with very nice curves. Not flashy, not bubbly, just stylish. She looked me straight in the eyes and I looked her back. She wasn't hard to look at.

"Yes, Shelly, what is it?"

"Miss Wilson, this is Mr. O'Keefe. He's got a problem and I don't want to call Mr. Wallace because you know how he is about these things and..." She started to cry.

"Just get to the point, Shelly." Miss Wilson appeared bored. She'd been down this road before.

"Maybe I can help." I stuck out my hand and she took it. Her grasp was firm and warm. "I'm Bill O'Keefe. I have some important information coming in on your fax machine and I need it tonight. Shelly is unsure how to handle it. She was thinking of holding onto the papers until tomorrow morning when the day manager comes in. I can't wait that long. The reason I came here was because I knew I could find the backup services I need to stay alive in my job over the weekend, otherwise I'd have gone to one of the local motels on the strip where it's cheaper." Miss Wilson gave me a professional smile, let go of my hand and glanced at the fax machine, churning out paper like a champ.

"You'll have to excuse Shelly. Most people are here on vacation." She pointed to the fax machine. "Give Mr. O'Keefe his papers, Shelly. The charges are listed in your procedures manual, pages 38-40, which you should have read and memorized before you came to work. Try doing that tomorrow instead of spending the day on the beach. Anything else I can do for you, Mr. O'Keefe?"

"You've been very kind, Miss Wilson. Maybe a drink and a little chat later if you're not too busy, thanks."

"I'm a very busy woman and we don't fraternize with the guests." She threw a glance at Shelly and gave me a real smile. "Thanks anyway. My office is just down the hall if you have any more problems."

Her smile would have rivaled the beauty of a morning sunrise and my heart jumped a beat. She disappeared down the hallway. It was a sight for these sore old lonely eyes just to watch her go. That's the ultimate test, you know. If a woman looks good coming and going then she's a good-looking woman. Yes, the moving test is the best and most accurate way to judge a woman's beauty and Miss Wilson had passed the test with flying colors. Unfortunately, I didn't have the time to become involved right now, especially on a case and there was no place for a woman in my present life. Shelly didn't appreciate Miss Wilson as much as I did.

"Boy! I hate this job!" She was leafing furiously through a large manual in a stiff brown binder. "What page was that?"

"Pages 38-40."

"Oh! No wonder. I thought she said pages 300-400. Boy, this is complicated. I hate that Miss Wilson. She's so damn smart. She couldn't just show it to me, could she? No! She just throws out some lousy numbers and struts off. She's a witch." Shelly suddenly looked up, as if she'd just realized she wasn't alone. "Oh, no. You won't tell her I said that, will you?" She looked at me with pleading eyes.

"Well, maybe, and maybe not. Here, let me see that manual. I'll figure it out for you and you can add it on my bill...Yes...It's fairly simple. Here, you see this? This is the computer entry format on page 39. Just type in those characters, add the amount and hit 'enter'." She got it right after several tries, with me doing most of it.

"That's easy. Why didn't Miss know-it-all Wilson tell me that?" She punched the "enter" key.

"Most things are simple once you've done them. Tell me more about this Miss Wilson." I reached over the counter, tore off the fax paper, and started separating the individual pages.

"That Miss Wilson is a real piece of work. She's from the main office in Chicago, some kind of whataya you call it, a compliance thing. Mr. Wallace owns the land but the Daylight people give us the stuff like the building, advertising, reservations, training and all that. So, Miss Stuck-Up Wilson works for them and she comes around here to make sure we do everything right. I hate it and so does Mr. Wallace. I only do this to get my tuition money so I won't have to stay in this crummy town another winter."

"So you live in East Harbour?"

"All my life and I hate it. I can't wait to get out of here. My parents love it. I don't know why. There's nothing here but seagulls and yuppies and I'm not in love with either one. They've ruined this town."

"The seagulls or the yuppies?"

"Who do you think? All those lawyers, doctors and bankers with their money and big ideas. Normal people can't live here any more."

"Sounds like you've had a rough time of it?"

"My father's a carpenter when he isn't fishing. I grew up with the sons and daughters of rich people. They had vacations while I had to work. They had tutors to get them through the tough subjects when I had to baby-sit, clean house and cook for my mom while she worked. I couldn't go to the senior prom because my mom got sick and couldn't make my dress. I had to stay home anyway to take care of the house and cooking and my five brothers and sisters. Then they passed all those zoning laws so nobody could build houses without paved roads, storm drains and minimum sized lots and we had to get approval from the conservation people, which never happens, so that put my uncle Tony into bankruptcy because all the land he owned was in restricted areas, made up by the Historical Commission and the Committee on Natural Resources or something and the wetlands thing and all of it is controlled by those stupid yuppies. They didn't ask Uncle Tony what he wanted and they never even gave a thought to what they did to us.

My uncle Tony and his two sons, my cousins Johnny and Frank, they all lost their houses and everything they owned and had to move in with us for a year. Then Mom got sick. That's what happens when the yukpuppies take over. The rest of us aren't smart enough to fight them off so they take over and do what they want. I'm not going to the beach tomorrow. I'm babysitting for my mom so she can go to work and pay bills until my dad can find work again. When I say babysitting, I'm not talking about sleeping late and watching TV all day. I'm talking about cleaning house, washing dishes, cooking and doing laundry. I hate this town. Any more questions?" There were tears streaming down her face so I waited for her to cool off before I started digging again.

"What's your last name, Shelly?"

"Cirelli. Shelly Cirelli. My father is Jimmy Cirelli. Do you know him?" She seemed to brighten a little.

"No, Shelly. I'll be honest with you. I don't know your father and I'm very sorry to hear what happened to your Uncle Tony and your cousins. That's not fair."

"No! It's not fair, so you can understand why I want to get out of here. I hate this place and I really hate what it's done to everybody."

"I can see that. You must know just about everyone in East Harbour. Maybe you can help me with something."

"You bet I do. Why do you ask?" She was suddenly wary.

"I'm interested in doing some business here and I just want to know what I'm getting into before I invest a lot of time and money."

"I'll bet you're here about the sewer project. That's going to bring a lot of jobs into town if it ever happens."

"Why wouldn't it happen?"

"Oh, I don't know. There's a lot of politics down at town hall and for a while it looked like it wasn't going to get done but that's all changed now."

"How's it changed? Did something happen that will change the sewer project?"

"Well...yeh. There was a man who was in control of the finances of the town and he was making everybody do things his way. He had a lot to do with the zoning and stopping the building here. He was a lawyer so he knew things a lot of us didn't know like what had to be done legal and all that. So, it was his idea to cut the costs on the sewer project by changing the financing to another bank or something. I think it was something to do about selling shares, or was it bonds or interest rates? There was something about consulting fees too. I don't really know. Anyway, he wanted the town to get outside contractors to bid so that us locals couldn't make any money on the work. This man, Mr. Berman, was making everybody pretty mad over the way he was doing things."

"Was that Murry Berman, by any chance?" She nodded. "I think I read where he died, didn't he? Did you know him?"

"Yeh, he's dead. He had an accident in his car. I didn't know him but my uncle built their house. Mr. Berman gave Uncle Tony a lot of trouble about that. He said there was water in the cellar or something. Big deal. Everybody's house has water in the cellar sometime. Then that Lydia Berman turned around and led the fight to stop development in East Harbour. She got Murry elected chairman of the finance committee and he cut the budget and laid off a lot of the local people who had jobs with the town. He put contracts up for bids so outsiders could come in."

"You seem to know a lot about this, Shelly."

"I've heard nothing else in my house since Murry Berman came to town and I'm sick of it."

"So, I take it you aren't upset about what happened to Murry Berman?"

"Mr. O'Keefe, Murry Berman got what he deserved. He was in the way." ❈

CHAPTER FOUR

t's amazing what people will tell a stranger. Until now I had no reason to believe Murry Berman might have been murdered. The hound dog in me wanted to know more but my mind wasn't focused. Miss Wilson left me feeling unsettled. "Never let 'em get to yah!" That's what my old partner, Willie Monk, always said. "Women is trouble enough widout you should make 'em do yourself more damage." So, when Shelly dropped the bomb about Murry Berman. I reacted too fast. Shelly wasn't so dumb after all.

"How was he in the way, Shelly?"

"I...I don't know. I shoulda never said that. I gotta get back to work. If I get anymore stuff for you on the fax, I'll leave it in your box."

"Yes...sure...Thanks. Well, I'll probably be sending and receiving quite a bit, so not to worry, and mum's the word about Miss Wilson, right?"

"Yeh, sure. Thanks." She excused herself and disappeared into a room behind the desk where a TV was playing. The interview was over.

There were fifty pages. I was hungry so I went to the dining room and found it deserted except for a bartender and waitress sitting together at the end of the bar. She was smoking a cigarette and he had his hand on her knee. I took a table in the far corner. The waitress finally tore herself loose and came sauntering over with a menu. She tried to act really sexy but the way she moved was comical, taking long swooping strides, as if she were on ice skates.

"Hi, I'm Sally. You wanna eat or just drinkin tonight, Honey?"

"Hi, yourself, Sally. I'm eating now, drinking later. What's good?"

"Not much." She tossed the menu on the table. "The seafood's frozen, comes from Canada. Veggies are microwaved. Potatoes are instant and the salads were made yesterday. Try the steak. Hank can't ruin the steak even if he tries and we just got a new sirloin strip in so it's gotta be good. Gonna have some myself before the night's out."

"Hank the cook?"

"Yeh, he's not really a cook. He's a construction worker or something, you know, drives a truck. Calls himself a carpenter but he's really more a foundation man when he's not driving truck. Since there's no more building going on around here he calls himself a cook but I know he does good steaks. I had one once." She winked at me.

"What cut is the best? New York sirloin, Delmonico, filet mignon?"

"All the same, just different prices."

"Okay, I'll have the New York sirloin. Make it a twelve-once cut and trim the tail. I don't want the tail."

"No tail anyway. Hank makes hamburger with them. Better stay away from the hamburgers. They're gross. I'll make sure he gives you a good steak. You'll have fries and corn with that. Want a fresh salad?"

"Sure."

"Dressing?"

"Italian!"

"Try the house. It's fresher."

"O.K., and a beer. Make it a Bud."

"You got it, Baby." She squinted at me, which must have been her smile, turned and swooped away, confident that I was watching her all the way to the kitchen. The girl had no class but she knew how to pump the tips. Put the cook down, rap the house, act like you're on the side of the customer. No wonder the place was deserted. A good manager would fire Sally and her bartender boyfriend. Never pays to have a couple running a bar. My beer arrived and I took a few moments to relax. It was a lounge and dining area combined. The carpet was a dirty brown and hadn't been cleaned. Imitation chandeliers, harpoons, fishnets and those imitation plastic figureheads made in Hong Kong decorated the wall. A small marlin, about three feet long was mounted in a flying leap over the bar. It wasn't even big enough to be called a game fish but it fitted into the general half-hearted sour salty dog mood of the place. Yet, if the food was edible, I could sit and review the files without wasting time.

I scanned the insurance application and affidavits, the statement by the salesman, a Frank Stillman, who wrote the policy, and the medical report by a Dr.Isadore Scram, the company's designated physician. I tried to decipher the doctor's handwriting and notes. Everything seemed in order: blood pressure 110/86, heart beat 84, blood type O-positive,eyesight 20/20, weight 185, figure trim, height 6'1", age 35. Murry Berman was a big man, in excellent health and his entire life ahead of him. Now he was dead and out of the way, whatever that meant. The underwriter's report and the approval of the policy were in order. The policy had been properly routed. Everything was there. The entire amount including the double indemnity clause had been accepted. Life insurance companies rate policies according to risk, and then decide which ones they want to keep. The higher risk policies are assigned to a risk pool, which is then underwritten by the companies in the industry. Any policy over $100,000 would normally be "laid off" to the pool. Berman's policy was squeaky clean, so State Mutual passed it through to the underwriter, Clinton Thornberger. He rated, approved and passed it on to be filed for normal processing by the file clerk in the secretary's pool. When this was over, Mr. Thornberger would be dead meat unless he could prove he was in Sandusky when Murry Berman's policy passed his desk.

I was trained as a commercial licensed underwriter, CLU, before becoming an investigator. I sold insurance, did the underwriting and supervised the whole process. I knew all the procedures and loopholes. I'd caught life insurance salesmen in all sorts of unethical and illegal acts, but this was a new one and it would take some hustle to find out what happened before the deadline for payment arrived. It was obviously an inside job and that was the first place I would start. No life insurance policy for $3 million with double indemnity for accidental death should ever have passed the supervisory level, let alone the underwriter's desk without someone questioning it. Harry Dondi said he was staying at the office all night and to call him for anything I needed. He wouldn't like what I wanted but that was just too bad. This baby wouldn't bankrupt the company but it would cause loads of trouble, which meant that Harry and many innocent people would be fired for something they didn't do. I'd known Harry for a long time and he was a decent man. He did me some favors and I liked doing business with him. Besides, he was honest and that was a rare item in this world.

The steak arrived and it looked so good I decided to eat it. Sally did her job. I'd give her a good tip and then go for whatever information I could get later when she was hooked. I dug into my meal like a hungry man should, ordered a second beer and wiped the plate clean, finished with a cup of coffee, cream and sugar, and was about to start on the paperwork again when a movement caught my eye. I pretended to be reading but the legs and perfume were too much, so I gave in and looked up into the blue-green eyes of Miss Wilson. I pride myself on being a cool hand under fire but something about this woman shook me.

"Mr. O'Keefe, I must talk with you."

"Why don't you join me, Miss Wilson?"

"The name's Connie," a hint of a smile passed her lips, "and this is not a social call, perhaps another time." She seemed to waver as she looked around the dining room. "No! I can't. Listen! We need to talk. Can you come to my office when you're through here? It's important."

"Yes. You bet...Is anything wrong, ahh, Connie?"

"Just come to my office. Take your time. Don't let anyone see you. I don't want to attract any attention." She turned abruptly and walked away. I followed her retreat with some degree of pleasure, but my curiosity and her agitated state caused the alarm bells to go off. I'd instinctively put my back to the wall at this corner table and now I was beginning to wonder if I should have found a place to stay out of town.

My old teacher, Willie Monk, always told me, "Billy, don't draw too much attention. Yah cuts down on your creditability and then yah gets less information out of people." He was a smart man. He never finished high school but he knew everything about investigating insurance fraud. I worked with him in the days before companies required a college degree just to fill out an application. Willie knew more about insurance fraud than any ten college graduates but the company decided that only diploma holders could catch crooks so they fired him. They said he didn't have the proper qualifications for the job so they offered it to me. I turned them down, quit, and went independent with Willie. We formed a partnership and in less than a year we had every big insurance company calling us for help. We could do things no internal investigators could do and we made big money, 10% of whatever we saved the company. No savings, no 10%. Then, a year ago, Willie got too old and too sick to do it anymore, so I carried on alone. He would have chewed me out royally for rushing into this thing with no preparation and no advance information. His words echoed in my mind. "Don't trust nobody. Don't take nobody for granted and don't never believe nothin' till you seen it for yourself wid your own eyes." I missed Willie and now the irony was, I was working for the company that fired him. Ahh, sweet revenge.

I took a few more minutes to leaf through the papers while finishing my coffee. Sally came over and tried to sell me some dessert but when I resisted, she handed me the check.

"I'll take that when you're ready, sweetie."

She lingered a moment as I took out a fifty and handed it to her.

"Keep the change, Baby. Looks like you can use it. Not much business for a Friday night."

"Thanks, you're a doll. It'll get busier later on when the drinkers come in. You should come back, unless your evening is occupied."

"Why would it be occupied?" I tried to act innocent.

"That woman, Miss Wilson! She a friend of yours?"

"You mean the one that just came in here?" I played dumb. "Didn't know her name. She just told me I had some messages. She didn't seem too friendly."

"Her? Friendly? She's a barracuda. I'd stay away from her if I was you. There's a lot more friendly girls in this town for a fellow like you, if you wanna have some fun?"

"Like who, for instance?" I was all innocence.

"Come back later and you'll see. I'll be here." She squinted a smile and swooped away with my fifty to the bar where the bartender was glaring at us.

I read a few more pages and came to the autopsy report. I found three items of interest and marked them with a red pen. First, there was glass embedded in Murry Berman's face and eyes. Some of it was windshield glass and some of it had been identified and analyzed by the coroner as, "...coming from the subject's eyeglasses which had also shattered on impact of his face with the steering wheel." The second was an excessive amount of adrenalin in Murry's blood. Not uncommon in cases of traumatic death except that Murry died instantly. They can tell from the amount of internal damage and bleeding, so there shouldn't have been much, if any, residual adrenalin in the bloodstream. Third, there was a residue in the stomach of six ounces of coffee, cream and sugar, with a donut. Hardly even a couple of swallows. There was no noticeable breakdown of the stomach contents, meaning that Murry's auto accident occurred during the drinking of his coffee.

Simple, O'Keefe, he was drinking a cup of coffee on his way to work while driving his car. So what's the big deal? Nothing complicated. My subconscious said, "Something is out of place here. File it away and keep an eye on it." Good advice. Willie Monk used to say, "Let yeh brains do its work. Feed it all the stuff yah got and then go to sleep or go fishin or stand on yeh head and let it so its own ting."

"So I packed up and left. People were filing into the lounge. There

were young men dressed in T-shirts, jeans and work boots and young
women with matching outfits except they wore sneakers. One young
lady, with a bust too big for her T-shirt, wore shorts and no shoes.
This was an anything-goes place. I would come back later and do
some digging, pump Sally for information while she was pumping
me for tips. "Give and get." That's what life is all about, but first, I
had a date with a barracuda. ❈

CHAPTER FIVE

I took Miss Wilson's warning seriously and slipped around the corner next to the front desk. The TV was blaring away in the office with Shelly glued to the tube, preparing herself for college and a meaningful life outside East Harbour. Down the hall to the left was the kitchen and stockroom. I opened the door to the right marked "MANAGER" and found an outer office with a small desk, file cabinets and a coffee maker on a table. I knocked twice on the door to the inner office, which stood open a crack and stepped inside where Miss Wilson was sitting at a desk in a larger room. Filing cabinets lined the left wall. A large, ornate teak desk with an ebony nameplate that read "Rick Wallace", sat in front of the far wall. There was a door to the left of the desk and teak bookshelves reaching floor to ceiling, going all the way up the wall and running around the corner to the right. Very impressive.

"Hello, I was afraid you weren't coming."

"You said to take my time. I didn't want to appear too eager"

She smiled a genuine smile. "I was afraid we were being watched. I thought you might go to your room or outside before coming here. Please, sit down." She still seemed upset.

"Why would someone be watching us?" I smelled her perfume as I sat down. Her hair reflected the light of the lamp behind her chair.

"It's complicated and frightening." She shuddered and began to sort through the papers on her desk. It was cluttered with computer runs and ledgers. A computer terminal occupied one corner.

"I must apologize for being so mysterious but I think you're about to step into something messy and dangerous with no idea what it is." She held up her hand. "Let me explain. I received a phone call from the Chief of Police, Myron Gates, warning me, on pain of going to jail, to notify him if you checked into this hotel. If you are here, he wants to know when you leave and come back, when you eat and when you sleep, and above all, who you talk to and what you say." She stopped and looked at me, her expression, troubled.

"And did you?"

"Did I tell him you were here?" I nodded. "No, absolutely not! I don't like Myron Gates but it's our policy to never help the local authorities spy on one of our guests. We've had some very bad experiences and I learned the police aren't always to be trusted."

"That's for sure." I smiled. She smiled.

"So, I have a confession to make. I hope you'll understand and allow me to explain before saying anything..." She picked up a stack of papers. "You may not be aware, Bill...by the way, may I call you Bill? This hotel and its parent company, Daytime Inns International, are owned by ATI, American Telex International, which in turn is solely owned by CFI, Continental Finances International. These two conglomerates have more connections than you can imagine. One of these is an information data branch containing records rivaling that of the FBI or any other major agency throughout the world. I took the liberty of 'running a make' on you. I know it's an invasion of your privacy and I apologize. I will give you this report and assure you there are no copies. It's just...well...I was frightened by what Myron Gates said and now I realize, after reading this report, that he deliberately misled me."

"What exactly did he say, Connie?"

"He said you were violent and to keep a very close eye on you. That you were dangerous and there were probably warrants out for your arrest someplace, that he would find them and when he did he would arrest you. He said you came here to start trouble and must be stopped."

"Well, he's partly correct. I am dangerous to some of the people in this town and they have an interest in watching me. I can assure you I'm not here to hurt anyone, especially you. Actually, I had something else in mind for the two of us."

"I can imagine," she laughed, "but it will have to wait. I want you to understand that Myron V. Gates is not someone to play around with. The sick joke here in town is that his middle initial, "V", stands for vicious. He's been accused of beating some of the kids in town so badly they had to be hospitalized and in one case a tourist, who was stopped for speeding by Myron, disappeared and was never heard from again. The state police, the FBI and the man's family looked everywhere but they found nothing. The town is a time bomb. It's ticking and any small spark could make it to go off. I'm afraid you might just be that spark. I wouldn't want that to happen. They've needed someone like you for a long time but it's not a job you can handle alone."

"I can handle myself, Connie. That's the business I'm in, intruding where there's fraud and deception but I'm just an insurance investigator, so I'll stick to insurance fraud and ignore the local politics."

"How about murder? You really don't know these people. They're scared and desperate. The two major factions in town are the locals on one side who have controlled everything for as long as they can remember. On the other side are the yuppies, the new arrivals that are mostly upper middle class professionals: doctors, lawyers, bankers, stockbrokers and financiers. They are literally at war, except the shooting hasn't started yet. The battleground has been the town hall and its committees where decisions mean jobs and contracts for the locals versus lower taxes and a protected lifestyle for the newcomers. This is no game for amateurs. It's a struggle to the death for both sides."

"I'm no amateur, Connie. Life is a battlefield and we learn as we go or we don't survive. I don't like what you're telling me and chances are I won't have to deal with any of it, but if I have to, I will."

"I believe you." She looked at the fax report in her hand. "William Thackery O'Keefe, father of three, two boys and a girl, divorced, freelance insurance investigator, Vietnam veteran, Special Forces, specialty-classified." She looked at me. "What does that mean: Classified?"

"It means there were things we did in Vietnam that we don't talk about. I was a professional then. I still am but I don't do those things any more. Only, I can take care of myself if I have to. Unfortunately, our society doesn't have any place for fellows like me with skills that we don't talk about, so I do what I can on a freelance basis, collect my 10%, then go back to my boat and go sailing, because it's a lot easier and safer for a guy like me to be alone."

"I'm sorry...truly I am sorry. I didn't mean to pry...its just, well, I like to know what I'm dealing with and Myron Gates really scared me. I asked John Chusak, our head of security in Chicago, for this report on you. He laughed and said to 'look out' when I gave him your name. He said you'd done work for us in the past and you were the best. He also said 'hello'. I'm really embarrassed." She handed the report to me. "Sorry." The barracuda had turned into a salmon, a beautiful, mysterious fish. Bad analogy O'Keefe but I like salmon. They're strong, loyal and they swim against the tide.

"Thanks, under the circumstances I don't blame you. I'd have done the same. I want to be honest with you because I need your help. You may not want to give it, and that's all right too. About what I did in Vietnam: I was a specialist in cutting-out operations. That means we went into enemy territory and kidnapped or killed key people on the other side: generals, politicians, community leaders in Hanoi and others. Sometimes we assassinated people in the middle who posed a threat to our operations by giving information to the enemy. It was a war and we thought we were right in doing what we did. We even had orders to justify it. I was very young then, not even twenty when I started, but I felt ninety when I got out. Now, I'm not so sure what we did was right even though we were just following orders, but I'm still very good at it. If you want me to help, I'll need your cooperation. I need to know who is who and where the battle lines are drawn and why Myron Gates is so worried about me? If you can help, I promise you I'll do my best to keep it clean, and I'll be out of the way in just a few days. You don't have to help if you don't want to, because if it gets dirty, you may see a side of me you won't like."

"I think I understand." She hesitated. The light played on her auburn hair and I began to imagine what she would look like on the boat in a setting sun.

"There's a part of me that likes excitement and you excite me..." She blushed, "I mean...well, you know what I mean...and so I'll do what I can to help. Besides, it's about time someone did something to shake these people up. They act like you can't touch them. They're arrogant and stupid. I'm from the Midwest, a small town in Iowa, you'll never guess the name."

"I think I can. Wilson, Iowa! Right?"

She blushed again. "Yes, Wilson, Iowa, a small town where everyone knows everyone. I'm not used to the sort of bullheaded ignorance that exists here in East Harbour. Oh, we had our trouble-makers in Wilson, but nothing like Myron Gates or Rick Wallace. Everyone gave way for the other person. We all respected other people's rights but that's not the way it is here."

"I come from a small upstate farming community and Myron Gates would never have been allowed to take a position of authority. I think it's the competition, combined with rapid change and too much growth. The locals probably think the yuppies have it made and the yuppies envy the simplicity of the locals' life style. It results in dirty politics and in-fighting and decent people don't want to get involved. That leaves it to the bad guys, but this same battle is going on all up and down the eastern coastline, so what's so different here in East Harbour?"

"I can give you a running history of this town, as far as I know it, but I don't see why you would want it. You are here to investigate an insurance policy, so why would you want to know all this other stuff?"

"I'm here to find out if there has been any fraud regarding the issuance of a life insurance policy on Murry Berman. My curiosity has been aroused now and I'm wondering if maybe murder and fraud exist side by side. Anything I learn can help solve the case."

"Okay, well, first you should know there are three families in town that count: Gates, Wallace and Cirelli. The people in this town always did as they pleased until city people came out and started a building boom. Local fishermen and farmers suddenly became expert carpenters. Farmland and swampland that was worthless became prime building lots. The families who owned land made money and there were jobs for many who had been out of work for years. Tax money flowed into the town treasury and the town fathers, who used to hold office just to have something to do, found themselves presiding over millions. They gave jobs and contracts to friends and relatives and also paid themselves quite well. The newcomers, like Murry Berman, didn't take long to catch onto what was happening and they started getting involved in the town's business. They revised the town's charter and Calvin Kinderhook became mayor. The locals resented him but he kept things under control so there were no more secret deals and spending came under stricter controls. The three selectmen were from the local families."

"So, how did Murry Berman fit into all this?"

"The Bermans came from the city. Murry was a corporate lawyer, not a very dynamic man but he had Lydia behind him and she's enough to drive any man, no matter how docile he might be. The house they bought is in a development started by the Cirelli brothers. The lot sizes were substandard. It was an area, which should have been designated conservation wetlands. The septic systems were too small and the land was too low with poor drainage. It was part of the old Gates potato farm but potatoes and houses aren't the same. One needs water, the other doesn't. There was water in the cellars, septic systems failed, wells became polluted, foundations settled, walls cracked, roofs leaked, roads flooded and washed out in the rainy season and cracked and fell apart when it was dry. Accusations, lawsuits, threats and counter-threats flew all over. The yuppies gained the upper hand when Murry Berman was elected chairman of the zoning board and building substandard houses on swampland was stopped forever. Next, Murry moved up to the finance committee and he trimmed the budget so tight many of the locals and their relatives lost their cushy jobs, and outside contractors were allowed to bid on town projects. Berman really wasn't liked by the locals after that, but everyone knew it was Lydia who was pulling his strings."

"Calvin Kinderhook told me about the spider web at the finance committee meeting. That evidently made Murry even more unpopular."

"That's for sure. Murry's fear of spiders was a liability that could have derailed the yuppies' bid to take control of town government. They still supported him in spite of it, however, because he was in the best position. He was being groomed to take over one of the selectman's positions. The selectmen are the bosses of the town. Myron Gates and all the others work for them. Of the other two selectmen, one is Ken Wallace and the other Frank Honey, a professor of Business Administration at Long Island College. The third is Merv Gates, Myron's grandfather. His term is expiring. The yuppies would have won the war if Murry had lived."

"So, Murry Berman ends up dead and the locals keep control of their town and their jobs?"

"Right! Until you showed up, so be careful. You may be their next target."

"Yes, but if all they wanted to do was knock Murry Berman off, why the insurance scam? It only draws attention and it's a dumb move. Do you know a Frank Stillman?"

"He's the local insurance tycoon. Stillman and Wallace Insurance. He's forever trying to sell me life insurance. Rick Wallace, his partner, owns this hotel, at least he does on paper."

"Can you describe Frank Stillman?"

"He's tall, thin, late thirties, brown hair and eyes, dark complexion. I think his mother was Portuguese.

"Does he wear glasses?

"No."

"He wrote the life insurance policy on Murry Berman."

"That fits. He'd sell insurance to a corpse if he thought he could get away with it."

"In a sense, he did. Murry Berman is dead and buried."

"Don't be ghoulish."

"Sorry. Say, would you mind doing me a favor?"

"Depends."

"I need to make a call. I'll use my credit card."

"No problem. I'll leave the room."

"Not necessary. I'll just be a minute." I dialed the phone and put it on speaker. Harry Dondi answered.

"Harry, this is Bill. Ready to copy?"

"Go."

"I need cross checks: Frank Stillman and Rick Wallace, both in the insurance business, Myron Gates, Chief of Police. Check all surnames Gates, Wallace and Cirelli against East Harbour addresses and I want you to check every name in underwriting and risk assignment as well as the secretary's pool to see if any of them has a connection with the deceased, the sales agent, the doctor or anyone else."

"You're crazy. A computer run like this will take forever. I'll have to call in extra help and camp out here all weekend. How am I going to justify all this overtime?"

"Try six million dollars, Harry?"

"Yeh, well, you got a point there. All right. Anything else?"

"Yes. I have the potential of some legal troubles brewing. Get me a court order to see the car and all police records. Keep Saul Goldstein on call, just in case I need him."

"Boy, Saul is gonna love this. Lawyers charge double on Labor Day weekend. Is that all or should I have the dog catcher in East Harbour checked for fleas?"

"You're a funny guy Harry. One more thing, run a check on a Miss Connie Wilson from Wilson, Iowa, and be careful, she doesn't like insurance agents."

"Who does? Okay, I'll get right on it. Be careful."

"Good night, Harry." I hit the disconnect button.

"So, you're going to run a check on me, huh?"

"Of course, I don't like surprises." We laughed and I left feeling good. Connie Wilson was a lady you'd be proud to take home to momma. It had been a long time since I felt this way about a woman and I was going to enjoy it as much as possible. The lounge was beginning to hop. The drinkers were drifting in and out and the music was blaring a hard rock song. The TV in the office was still going as I went outside to pick up my briefcase. Now that I look back on it, I was very lucky. My car was parked in the first row, directly under a street light less than twenty yards from the front entrance and there were no other cars near it. Most of the lounge crowd had parked around the side of the building where there was less light, the better to hide what you're doing in the back seat.

I opened the Caddy's trunk, put the car keys back in my pocket, opened my briefcase, dropped the Murry Berman file into it, closed the briefcase, put it on the ground and closed the trunk. I was aware of all sorts of strange noises in the night, but dismissed them because this was an unfamiliar place. It was a cloudless, dark night and my back was to the wind. A cool sea breeze was blowing from the south off the ocean at about ten knots. I could feel the pounding of the surf several blocks away. Then I realized it wasn't the surf. It was the sound of running feet and I saw them coming at me as I closed the trunk. ❄

CHAPTER SIX

I t was a poorly planned attack by a bunch of amateurs in hunting boots and flannel shirts. They were waiting for me behind the bushes in front of the hotel. It's a big mistake to come at your victim across an open lighted space of twenty yards with clodhoppers pounding. They were strung out in a ragged line, the last one leaving his bush as the first was only a few yards away. The first attacker headed to my left around the front of the car, while the others went right.

I dropped the briefcase, moved left, met the point man with a flying kick to the chest and flattened him on his back. Then I kicked him in the head just like a kicker kicks the ball on a Sunday afternoon pro football game. He didn't move after that. I met the second attacker the same way with a chest kick, which put him down temporarily, but I didn't have time to finish him off, because the third one came at me with a flying tackle. I barely avoided him by lifting my left leg, allowing him to pass by. The forth attacker was huffing and puffing along, still coming and no immediate threat, so I turned to face the other two.

They came at me with long pointed deadly knives, and we circled, them trying to get their nerve up and me trying to figure out what to do next. I decided to take out the one on the left after the second circle. He was taller and looked to be slower. Besides, I'd already kicked him in the chest once. I remember thinking, 'Why not finish the job'? I feinted at the short guy on the right and lashed out with my left foot, jabbing at the bigger man's left knee. There was a crunching, snapping of cartilage and ligaments and a howl of pain. The little one on the right came at me too fast and before I could jab him with my right foot, he was swinging his knife down in a lethal arc at my neck. I parried his blow with my left arm and chopped viciously with my right at his neck. I only got a piece of him but it was enough to put him down on one knee and I hit him again, this time across the back of the neck and followed it up with a kick to the ribs. He went down and out.

My instincts warned me to keep moving. I spun around and squatted down presenting as little profile as possible. I saw a movement behind the car and I recognized him as he stuck his pin head up to see where I was. I was blinded by the muzzle flashes of three shots fired in quick order. They missed by a mile but the effect was startling. I rolled to my right and charged the car. He was gone, running across the parking lot, my briefcase in one hand, gun in the other, huffing and puffing as he went. That happens when big overweight men try to run. There wasn't anything in the briefcase that couldn't be duplicated and I knew where to find him. The other three on the ground were just beginning to stir.

I frisked them, taking their I.D.'s. There were two guns, another knife and some brass knuckles. Shelly was coming through the front glass doors with Connie Wilson behind her as I dumped the spoils of war into my trunk. The look on Connie's face said it all. She wasn't accustomed to bodies and bullets in her hotel parking lot.

"Bill! Oh my God, Bill! You're bleeding!"

Blood was dripping down my left arm. Connie was looking at the slit in the left shoulder and sleeve of my sports jacket. The little guy got me as he went down. Other people were coming. Shelly was crying uncontrollably and Sally, the waitress, went running from body to injured body making funny little squeaky noises. Connie wrapped a scarf around my arm and it started to hurt. I felt light-headed. There were halos around all the lights and a buzzing in my ears. I felt terrible.

"Connie!" I whispered in her ear. "Get me outta here. Act casual but get me to a place I can lay down, fast!" She didn't hesitate.

"Follow me!" she said grabbing my good arm.

We went off to the left, just like a couple of people walking to the hotel lounge. We went round the back, in a service entrance to the kitchen, then through the stockroom, out a door and down a corridor to another door. Connie had a key.

"In here. You'll be safe. Nobody ever comes here."

We were in a room with a couch. The kitchen, to the right, was separated by a bar and a pass through window from a dining area. Abstract paintings covered the walls.

"Straight ahead, Bill. You'll be safe here. Nobody ever comes to my apartment." Connie led me down a hallway with a bedroom on the left and into a bathroom with a hydro spa and a sauna on the right.

"Pretty nice place," I mumbled, feeling even worse.

"Shut up and sit down you big lug. You're bleeding."

"I'm all right. Just a little scratch."

Connie pulled the jacket off and tore the sleeve of my shirt. She gasped and the sudden look of shock on her face told me it was bad.

"You have to see a doctor. This is really bad."

I glanced in the mirror at a deep gash about eight inches long, straight down the back of my upper left arm. Not a pretty sight and it was bleeding profusely.

"Have you got a needle and thread?" I began unbuttoning my shirt with my right hand. I couldn't feel my left hand.

"You must be kidding? If this gets infected you could die. I grew up on a farm, and I've seen these things before."

"I can't afford to go to a doctor. Myron Gates was one of them. This conflict just turned into a shooting war." I was getting dizzy. The room started a slow spiraling turn to the right.

"Call Harry Dondi," I mumbled, and the lights went out.

The next thing I remembered was daylight coming through a window. Everything looked strange. My mouth was very dry and I had a fierce headache. My left arm and shoulder were throbbing with each heartbeat. Must be in a hospital...yeh, a hospital. Curtains on the windows, flowered wallpaper, a dresser with makeup, hairspray, little figures of dancing angels on a doily, and a closet with double louvered doors. The nightstand to my left had a lamp and a telephone. An easy chair was in the far corner, a brass floor lamp behind it and a pair of woman's high-heeled shoes on the rug. Thought hospitals had tile floors so they could be washed and scrubbed. Hospitals smell funny too. This place didn't smell bad. Actually, it smelled pretty good. My head wasn't working too good so I shook it: big mistake! Felt like somebody was pounding on my brain, and when I shook it, all the marbles inside banged around and made me sorry I was alive, but it worked.

Now I remembered. There was a fight. No! It was an Indian attack. There were...let me think...ouch...three, no four of 'em. Yeh and I kicked butt. Man I really did a number on 'em. Yeh.

"So," said a little voice way down deep. "So! Tell us something O'Keefe, if you kicked butt so good, why are you here feeling so bad?"

"Simple," I said out loud to the stupid little voice inside. "I got stabbed with a dirty fishing knife and it bled a lot and got infected. Then I died."

"What did you say?" Connie Wilson sat to my right in a straight back chair.

"I said...Oh never mind...how long have you been sitting there?"

"Since the doctor left." She looked at her wristwatch. "About midnight I guess. That would make it ten hours, right?"

She felt my forehead. Her hand was cool and soft and I sensed a faint stirring in my gut in spite of the pain. Ah yes, my mind began to remember Miss Connie Wilson, my guardian angel. Nice thoughts.

"Was I much trouble?"

"No more trouble than a raging bull in a china shop."

"Sorry, I didn't intend for you to get this deep into it."

"No problem, O'Keefe. I was having a dull life anyway. Besides, it did my heart good to see our friend, Myron Gates, come unglued in front of half the town. He never expected to see three of his own deputies lying on the ground in front of this hotel. He wanted to know where you were, and why your car was here if you weren't, and what was your room number? I didn't tell him anything but our helpful desk clerk, Shelly Cirrelli, squealed on you. He turned the hotel upside down, smashing doors and trashing rooms, so I called Chicago, and our legal department told him to get out or face charges for trespassing, breaking and entering and violation of six or seven civil rights laws I didn't even know existed. I'm preparing a bill for the damages which will be sent to the town."

"Did he try to search this apartment?"

"No one but Rick Wallace knows about this apartment. The entrance is hidden. I had the locks changed and metal clad security doors installed. I keep sensitive and confidential information in my desk over in the corner, and I don't want anyone looking at it. Shelly thinks I live in Rick Wallace's office. I try not to be friendly with any of them. I have a job to do here and the fewer friends I make, the easier it will be in the end."

"What does that mean?"

"It means we're thinking of closing down this hotel. Rick Wallace is an incompetent playboy who drink's, sniffs cocaine and chases skirts. The place would be bankrupt if I wasn't here. Before I came in last year, he had his hands so deep in the cash register, he was six months behind on his franchise lease payments. We could have taken it away from him then, but no one really knew what the room and food take was, so it was decided to put a watchdog audit on Wallace and his hotel to see if it was worth taking over. My recommendation is to shut it down and get out with whatever we can realize from a sheriff's sale."

"Does Rick know all this?"

"I explained it all, but he's determined no one can touch him. He says it's his land and nobody can take it away. All the land on the western side of East Harbour was the Wallace Potato Farm and Rick grew up working for his father and grandfather. He started selling the land and living the good life after they passed away. He acts almost omnipotent. I've never seen such blind arrogance."

"It's probably the drugs. You'll see a lot of agitation and paranoia in the advanced stages of addiction. Not a pretty sight, and dangerous."

"I've no experience with this sort of thing. I take it you have?"

"My experience with druggies and alcoholics has taught me to cut my losses. They seldom get clean or straight."

"This thing scares me. I never dealt with people like these. If it wasn't for you, I'd call Chicago and tell them to get me out of here."

"That might be a good idea. Looks like we're dealing with outlaws. Your silent struggle between the locals and yuppies just left the rooms of the town hall and committee meetings and turned into a shooting war, and we're in the middle of it all."

"This was a desperate attack. There must be a lot at stake?"

"They were stupid. They didn't know what they were up against. Next time they won't be so careless."

"You won't have to worry about Howie Cash and Joey Cirelli. They have major head injuries and internal bleeding. Howie has a broken neck, a punctured lung and he's paralyzed from the shoulders down. Joey had a cardiac arrest. They revived him, but he's on a breathing machine. I heard the medics say Joey's whole chest is just a mess of broken bones. Hank Wallace, Rick's cousin will never walk on that knee again. You did all that damage, and all you got was a little scratch on your arm," she teased.

"You said these fellows were Myron Gates's boys?"

"They're all local men, what are called reserve policemen. They put on a uniform when there's a parade or the road is torn up. It's one of the jobs the locals keep for themselves. This is a small town with part-time police and firemen. It's more like a club but they make good money. Murry Berman was planning to put an end to that by hiring what he called 'real policemen' and 'real firemen'."

"So, I was attacked by the local police force, East Harbour's finest?

I should have gone for the little guy first. He was too fast."

"What?" Connie was brushing her hair. Looking at me in the mirror.

I reached out and touched her neck. She didn't draw away from me.

"That was Howie Cash. He was a Marine."

"Figures." I stroked the back of her head.

"You must be feeling better."

"I feel like hell, but you make me feel like a million."

"I do my best; sir, but you were a bit too much for me last night."

"I don't remember. Was I good?"

"Well, you passed out sitting on the edge of the hydro spa. I couldn't hold you, so I laid you on the floor and wrapped a towel around your arm. It bled something awful. You must weigh two hundred pounds!"

"One ninety." I ran my hand through her hair.

"Yes, so I took your advice and called your friend, Harry Dondi. He said he'd have a doctor here in about a half hour. I found you trying to stand up when I came back. You didn't know me and before I could get there, you fell backwards and hit your head on the corner of the sauna bench. I thought you were dead, Bill. I honestly thought you had died. You broke the bench with your head." She stopped brushing and stared at me in the mirror.

"That explains my headache." I felt the large lump on my head.

"You bled so much I didn't know what to do. Dr. Smith arrived. He was on vacation at the beach. I brought him in the back way, a pretty tough thing with Myron Gates and his men all over the place. The doctor's coming back at noon today."

"I can hardly wait. I need to get out of here, go to work." I tried to sit up. The throbbing in my head increased.

"You're being stupid. Stay there or I'll hit you on the head again." I got one leg over the side of the bed, levered myself up and dangled my legs. I realized I was naked with only a sheet draped across my lap.

"Where are my clothes?" I tried to cover myself with a blanket.

"They're being cleaned and washed, so lay back down and relax. You can't go any place without them."

"Who took them off?" I saw a grin spread across her face.

"You bled a lot and your clothes were a mess. The doctor had problems stopping the bleeding. We put you in bed and I cleaned you up. I did what had to be done." She was still grinning.

"So, tell me Connie, was I a gentleman?" I wasn't feeling well.

"Oh yes. You handled it all very well." She wasn't smiling any more. The room was starting to turn and my brain was buzzing.

"Are you all right?" She grabbed my good arm.

"I think I'll just lay down again," I mumbled. The dizziness and nausea passed as the room slowed down and finally stopped spinning

"There! You see? You aren't well. You lost a lot of blood and that lump on your head is the size of an orange, so relax and take it easy." The room came into focus again and I could see her beside the bed, the silhouette of her figure framed in the light of the window, her white cotton blouse tucked into faded jeans held tight by a braided rope belt around her waist. I wasn't too sick to notice that she was a very attractive woman. Her auburn hair brushed her shoulders as she moved, reflecting the sunlight like the autumn leaves of a maple tree. I was almost in a trance as I lay there watching her.

"Furthermore, my friend," she went on, "I agreed to help you because I thought you were doing the right thing, coming into the town and investigating the death of a man that a lot of people didn't like. I thought maybe you would shake things up and find a way to get this town moving in the right direction so there wouldn't be so much bickering and in fighting. This hotel isn't doing well because of the people's ignorant attitude. Tourists come to East Harbour one time and they never come back because of the treatment they receive."

"I think I experienced some of that."

"Yes and it's got to stop or the town will resemble a 17th century Salem Village with witch trials and hangings. Myron and his so-called deputies make too much money off parking tickets and traffic violations. People won't even shop here for fear of having their cars towed."

"I never heard much about East Harbour."

"Much of this is recent. As the locals lost money and jobs from

budget cuts, they tried to make it up in other ways. They've killed
the golden goose and don't realize it. The newcomers won't give up
and move out no matter how rough it gets and the old-timers can't
readjust."

"I'm beginning to understand." I was feeling better, so I sat up
and propped the pillow behind my back. "I came here to check out
a possible case of insurance fraud and instead I've stepped into the
middle of a class war with guns, knives and all the trimmings. I'm
not sure where to begin. If I was smart, I'd just call Harry Dondi and
tell him to get someone else, collect my expenses and go sailing." I
could see the disappointment cloud her face. "But I'm not that smart,
so I guess I'll stay around and keep digging." Connie gave me a kiss
and I kissed her back.

"Thanks. I guess I was wondering what you were planning to
do. It's been lonely living here and working with Rick Wallace. I
really don't care to get involved with the yuppie crowd, so I keep to
myself."

"It's not good to be alone."

"Is that a personal or professional opinion?"

"Both, I suppose."

"Being alone can be safer and as long as I work at this hotel.
Safety is a big consideration."

There was a knock on the door and Connie went out to the living
room to answer it. She returned, followed by a small man dressed
in dark slacks, a plaid sports jacket, dark green golf shirt, alligator
on the pocket: country club dress. He wore spectacles and carried a
small black bag.

"This is Dr. John Smith. He saved your life last night."

"I think Connie's exaggerating, but thanks anyway." He looked at
me over his spectacles and frowned. He was a young man, perhaps
in his early thirties. We shook hands.

"Actually, Mr. O'Keefe, she saved your life. She stayed with you and
slowed the flow of blood. It's a good thing or you would be resting
in the county morgue." He rummaged through his bag, coming out
with a stethoscope.

"Sit up straight and breath deeply...say ahh." He thumped me on the chest and back, looked into my eyes, examined my left arm, and carefully removed the bandage. It was blood stained and Connie let out a loud gasp when he pulled it loose.

"Nasty cut. Had a time of it trying to stop the bleeding. Don't like doing this sort of thing outside a hospital but Harry Dondi's a good friend. He insisted that we keep it confidential. Can't say I'm too happy but he spoke highly of you." He squeezed. "Does that hurt?"

"Yes!" My eyes watered from the pain. "You can stop any time."

"You're a very lucky fellow. Bleeding's stopped, stitches holding, no sign of infection. Very lucky for you considering the size of that cut and with a fish knife. You're a fast healer and it looks like you've had a few other wounds, some of them gun shots. I don't know about you people. Tough way to make a living. Course, compared to the three fellows you tangled with, you got off easy." He changed my bandage, gave me a shot, checked my blood pressure and packed his bag.

"You were a couple of pints low when I got here so I had to give you a transfusion. You're all right now."

"I hope you had that blood tested, Doc. I'd hate to catch something from a blood transfusion." He looked at me, then at Connie.

"Didn't she tell you?" Connie looked embarrassed.

"It was her blood. I had nothing else and she was compatible. You're a lucky fellow. You better hang onto this lady." He picked up his bag and walked out. ❄

CHAPTER SEVEN

onnie made chicken soup with the thin noodles, Penn-sylvania Dutch style, like grandmother used to make. She added stone ground crackers, Vermont cheddar cheese and a cup of strong tea. Normally, I don't eat pansy food like this but I was hungry and the warmth of the soup and tea recharged my vitals. Doc Smith left some painkillers, so I took a couple and I felt pretty feisty, as in let's get out of bed and get dressed.

"Your suitcase was in the hotel dumpster. The briefcase was empty on the ground about fifty feet away. One of our janitors found it half an hour ago. Too bad you didn't leave those papers with me." Connie brought the suitcase over to the bed. "I think maybe you should wash up first." She smiled and left the room, closing the door behind her.

It took awhile to get it all together. The hard part was putting on my shirt. I had some mobility with my left arm but not a lot, so I had to put my left shirtsleeve on first, which I normally don't do. It was harder than I thought and I was almost exhausted by the time I finished. Whenever I travel, I always pack a casual change of clothes, which I was now wearing. I would blend in with the summer population better but there were a few things I didn't have. I needed some armament and it's always easier to hide a weapon under a sports jacket or coat. I had to return to my cottage and pick up my 9mm Beretta and a good knife. For now I was casual. Later I'd be dressed formally, so to speak, and the next jerk that took a shot at me would be sorry. I came out of the bedroom feeling refreshed and determined to get on with the case only to find Connie talking to a long-faced Harry Dondi.

"O'Keefe! My God man! You look terrible. Why, you're walking like a zombie. Here, sit on the couch." He reached out to take my left arm and I pulled away from him.

"You sit on the damn couch, Harry. You're the one not looking so good." I brushed his hand aside and went to the kitchenette, picked up a glass and filled it with water. Connie followed.

"Are you Okay, Bill? Harry came on his own to see if you're all right."

"No problem, babe. This is just the way friends talk to each other." I turned and looked at Harry.

"Look! Bill. I honest to God didn't know what was going down here. If I'da known I woulda sent in more troops and warned everybody. I'm really sorry. I just came down to salvage what we got so far."

"So, Harry!" I took a slug of water from the glass to give myself time to calm down. "What you're saying is you knew these people were dangerous and you didn't warn me because you were afraid I wouldn't do the job? Now you're really worried because it's Saturday afternoon and nobody else is available until Tuesday, the first day after Labor Day, and probably not even then, because the only investigators you've got are wimpy, college graduates, ex-insurance salesmen, suck-butts turned snoops, and you wouldn't dare send them into a nutcracker like this."

I took another slug of water, rolled it around in my mouth to fight the dryness and swallowed. My body was dehydrated.

"Geez, Bill. You really know how to hurt a friend. I come all the way down here to see how you are and you insult me by accusing me of something as underhanded as that. I gotta tell yah, I was really shocked when this beautiful lady here called and told me what'd happened. I never dreamed anything like

this would go down. So here I am...you see me in the flesh...
what can I do for you? Geez, Bill. Please? Speak to me."
 "You can answer some simple questions." I finished off the glass of
water. "O.K. Harry?" He nodded. "Good. First of all, did you run a
background report on Murry Berman and East Harbour before you
called me?"

"Well...ahh...gee..."

"Cut the crap, Harry. That's the first thing. That's where you get
the basic stats like name, address, phone number, age, sex, etc. So
tell me why didn't you include those background reports in the stuff
you sent me? It wasn't there, Harry!"

"Well, ahh, I don't really know, Bill. Ahh...it must have been overlooked or maybe it got lost in transmission or somethin'."

"So, what did the report say, Harry?"

"I don't really remember but I'll dig it up when I get back."

"Yeh, you do that, but now you're here, what say I refresh your
memory a little. Like the town of East Harbour, Harry? What's the
bond rating on East Harbour?"

"Oh, it's not too good, Bill." He looked around the room.

"How bad is it, damn you?"

"Oh...ahh..."

"Is it a 'B' rating?"

"No...ahh...worse than that."

"C?"

"Ahh...yeh! About that, maybe a little under a 'C' rating."

"And the history of claims against insurance companies by the
town and it's employees?"

"Ahh...not too good, I'm afraid. Lots of casualty and disability
claims."

"And what's the rating, listed in the County and State Municipal
Rating Services Book? You know what I mean: fire, police, roads,
schools?" Harry was sweating.

"Lousy, just, lousy. Only data we have is two years old but this is
one of the worst run towns on the island. Hell! It's one of the worst
in the state!"

"And Murry Berman's background report. It indicated he was

involved very deeply in the town government and it's finances. Yes, Harry?" He nodded. "So, Murry Berman ends up dead with a three million dollar, double indemnity life insurance policy less than three months old, and you send me in here to investigate, and you don't tell me anything about a connection between the rotten town politics and the insured. What would Willie Monk say, Harry? What did Willie always say, damn it? Speak to me." I was right up in his face at this point.

"Yeh...O.K., Bill. Willie always said no piece of information, no matter how small or insignificant, should be overlooked."

"Right, that's rule number one, Harry, and now what was Willie Monk's rule number two?"

"Always study the connections. Who talks to who?"

"And rule number three?"

"Oh hell, Bill, don't do this to me. It's humiliating."

"That's right, you creep and you deserve it. It wasn't you they tried to kill last night. You didn't bleed a drop, Harry. I did the bleeding and it was your fault. Now what's rule number three?" Harry mumbled something. "Speak up Harry. Be a man!"

"O.K., O.K., rule number three is never trust the company. There! Are you satisfied?"

"Not really, Harry, but it's a beginning, you jerk. Is there anything else out of place here that I should know about before I step back out into that parking lot?" Now he was on a roll. Harry wanted to help.

"Yeh...there is something else. One of our internal investigators came up with something. There've been two large life insurance claims made here in East Harbour in the last three years. I don't have the names and all the details. You know what I mean?" I nodded and he continued. "Yeh...well...there was a man who disappeared here three years ago and his wife filed a claim, but then she withdrew it suddenly and they never found the body. The F.B.I., State Police and everybody was in on that one, but it was dropped. Then last year there was a drowning death. A large claim was filed and we paid it. I don't have all the details but I can send them to you if you think it's important."

"What do you think, Harry? Three deaths in three years in the same town all insured heavily by the same company? What the hell! Does that sound important to you? You didn't even think to let me know? What are the odds that three men, not men or women, but three men, all insured by your company would die accidental deaths in the same town in three consecutive years? I don't like being set up like this. You should know better. We were a team. You, Willie and me. We did it all and nobody ever got in our way so tell me what's going on? What's the real reason you're here? You didn't come down here just to see how I'm doing. You knew that already from Doctor What's His Name.

"Dr. Smith. I couldn't trust anyone else." He looked like a caged rat and tears were rolling down his cheeks so I decided to let up on him even though he didn't deserve it. He'd damn near got me killed.

"O.K. Harry. What's really going on?" I backed off.

"Oh, God, Bill. I told 'em you were too smart but they sent me here to talk you into a fixed retainer. Honest, it wasn't my idea but they made me come anyway."

"Who made you, Harry?" He looked down and scuffed the rug.

"I got a call from John Stanley in Omaha. He called me, Bill." Harry was very impressed. "I didn't call him. He told me to offer you a $25,000 retainer and to get someone else if you turned it down. He said if I couldn't handle it, he'd turn it over to someone else. They aren't bluffing. I'm sorry but he even sent a fax to back it up. Here, I've got it right here. It's got his signature on a letterhead from the president's office. He signed it himself, not one of those stamped repro signatures. He actually signed it himself." I waved it aside. "But, you can't turn this one down. It's too big. I need you. You can't just walk away from this."

I turned toward the bedroom and he followed me. I threw my suitcase on the bed and started tossing my meager possessions into it. I wasn't feeling well but it was time to leave.

"Bill! You'll regret this the rest of your life. No investigator ever walked out on State Mutual and lived to work again. You know that. It's worth $25,000. That's more than most people make in a whole year. All you have to do is find one little reason not to pay and we're off the hook. Any junior investigator could do this one."

I closed my suitcase, picked it up and walked past him. Connie was standing in the doorway of the bedroom. I walked over, put my good arm around her and planted a big juicy kiss right on her mouth. She was startled at first but picked it up and responded with a passion I didn't expect but certainly enjoyed. It felt damn good to have her in my arms. Make that in my arm.

"Isn't there some way you can help Harry out with this Murry Berman thing, Bill?" She had a point. Harry was still my friend even though he was weak in some areas.

"Look, Harry. I can take you off the hook. You won't have to pay the six million dollars to Lydia Berman. I could take the $25,000 and do the same, but I don't care about the money. No insurance company can afford to stiff an investigator this way and get away with it and John Stanley is going to find that out. So, I'll do you a favor and give you the clues you'll need to stop the payment of the claim on Murry Berman's death. It's very simple." Harry reached inside his jacket and came out with a small notebook and pen.

"You won't need to copy this down. First of all, check the insurance doctor's physical exam against the autopsy report. It's so obvious you could have caught it in-house without even calling me. The height, weight and blood type don't match and Murry wore glasses. The other thing is, Murry Berman was arachnophobic. He was terror-stricken by spiders. That's not listed in the medical questionnaire section of the agent's report or the insurance doctor's physical exam. So there you have it, Harry. All you have to do is run it by the legal department, send a letter to the grieving widow and you're a hero."

"That's fantastic. I'll see that you get paid the $25,000 anyway, Bill." Harry was writing furiously in his little notebook.

"No! No! No! Harry, read my lips. I'm giving this one to you to save your job. I work for a 10% commission or I don't work at all. I just want to go to my cottage in the dunes and heal. Then I'm going back to my boat for some serious sailing. I don't want the money and I don't ever want to work for State Mutual or John Stanley ever again. End of story and you can tell him so. Of course, he'll get the message when no decent investigator will work for him in the future, but that's another story."

"I owe you one this time. I don't know how I can ever thank you."

"I'll think of something. Take care and say hello to the family."

"You bet. Take care yourself." We shook hands and he left. I turned to Connie.

"I'm headed back to my place. I'd like to see you again."

"Any time, mister. Just give me a call."

"Walk me out." When we reached my car, Connie kissed me again in a way that said 'come back soon'.

"Take it easy for a few days, Bill. I'll be here. I want you in good shape the next time I see you."

"Sorry about all the trouble, lady."

I found my way to the center of town and followed the signs toward the highway. I made it two blocks when I heard the siren and saw the blue flashing lights behind me. I thought about not stopping but decided it might be better to finish it here and now. I left the motor running, put it in park and rested my hands on the top of the steering wheel.

"You wanna step out of there, Mr. O'Keefe!" Myron Gates stood slouched by my door, hand on his gun.

"You sure that's what you want, Myron?" I said without moving. I was feeling mean. Another car stopped behind the police cruiser. It was Harry Dondi. He got out and walked up to Myron Gates.

"Whad'ya want, mister?" Gates swung round, spread his fat legs and stood poised ready for an attack.

"He's with me, bird brain!" I'd had enough.

"What's the problem, officer? My friend, Mr. O'Keefe and I were just leaving town."

"Oh yeh?" Myron was very nervous.

"Yeh, Myron," I snarled, "I'm quitting. I'm leaving town. You won, so if you've got the slightest bit of intelligence, you'll leave it alone and count yourself very lucky. If you're really as stupid as I hope you are, I'll be only too happy to step out of this car right now and we'll settle it." He thought about it for a moment and there was a point when I thought he might give it a try but he stepped back, and looked at me with a meanness I'd only seen before in the eyes of wild animals.

"Another time, O'Keefe. I'm a patient man."

"No, shit head, there won't be another time. This is it. Leave it alone and don't ever try anything with me or mine ever again. Count yourself lucky. You ever try messing with me again and it will be the last time you mess with anyone." I took the parking ticket he gave me the day before and tossed it at his feet. He picked it up, gave me a look of disgust, walked back to his police cruiser, did a "u-turn" and drove away.

"Follow me out of town, Harry...and thanks, I owe you."

"Anytime. See you on the other side, friend."

"You bet." At the main highway, we waved and he went west to the city while I turned east towards home. I kicked it up to ninety mph and settled back.

"I got news for you, Myron Gates, Baby. There is definitely going to be another time and you will be sorry!" ✾

CHAPTER EIGHT

The cottage was just as I'd left it twenty-four hours before. The front door was locked with the key under the mat for anyone who needed to enter. No sense in someone breaking in. The place was part of my divorce settlement. My grandfather built the cottage and passed it down through the family. I never dreamed some judge would take it. In the end, after a very bitter battle, the judge generously gave me the boat and the summer cottage, and she got the house with two car garage, two Cadillacs, swimming pool, sauna and hot spa, stock portfolio, life insurance, savings accounts (hers and mine), safety deposit box, her jewelry, my gun collection, kids' stamp collection and my motorcycle. I couldn't believe it was happening as we sat there five years ago in the courtroom, Natalie on one side with her slick-chick feminist attorney, and me on the other with Saul Goldstein.

"I'm not a divorce lawyer, Bill. You should get yourself a good divorce attorney. They'll pick you clean." Saul did his best but it was more than just being a good lawyer that counted in that courtroom. A man had to be blind not to see something was going on between that judge and Natalie's lawyer, Selma Freidman.

Every time Saul stood up to object the judge told him to "shut up and sit down". Finally, I requested permission to ask a question and surprisingly the judge granted it.

"I want to know why she needs two cars and a motorcycle, your honor? What's she going to do, start a used car lot?" He yelled at me to "shut up and sit down", and so it went. The grounds for the divorce were stated as incompatibility. She tried for cruel and abusive treatment but it didn't stick. When she got on the stand and the judge asked her what I'd done to cause the divorce she said, "He quit his job and now I have to go to work to support the children and pay all the bills." Saul asked her what bills she was referring to, but she couldn't name them. He asked her how much was owed on the house and cars but she didn't know, and then the judge asked her what sort of work she thought she might do and she didn't know. Saul pointed out that the house and cars were paid for. The summer cottage was free and clear. The sailboat was paid for.

"There are no bills, your honor! So what's this all about?"

She answered, "He humiliated me. He quit his job. No man in my family has ever been unemployed." Saul countered that I went into business with Willie Monk. I wasn't out of work. I was always a good provider and now was in a better position than ever to support my family. The judge's response was to order me to pay ten percent of all my income in addition to five thousand dollars a month cash, child support and alimony, pay all the bills, life insurance, health insurance and oh yes, braces for the kids.

Then they threw a real weirdo at us. Natalie graduated from a very prestigious Boston women's college before we were married, but she never worked. Since she obviously had no skills and it was some time since she'd been in school, it was imperative that she return to college to study for her graduate degree and improve her marketable skills. And what degree would she be pursuing? Why of course, a P.H.D. in English Literature. What would she do with such a sophisticated degree? Why teach, of course, came the answer or perhaps she would become a writer, an editor or something like that, and oh yes, at least two years of that P.H.D. stuff would have to be done as a residency in old England herself, the source of the mother tongue. Childcare during that time would naturally have to be provided for at Mr. O'Keefe's expense.

"So, what d'ya think about that, your honor?" says Natalie's lawyer.

"Sounds good to me," says the judge.

"Objection!" says Saul Goldstein.

"Shut up and sit down!" says the judge

It never occurred to me that she really hated me until the very end when her attorney walked up to the judge and handed him a petition.

It said, "We pray the court take consideration of our petition, here entered, to seize said property now jointly held by one, William T. O'Keefe and wife, Natalie M. O'Keefe, formerly one Natalie M. Sullivan of Scarsdale, N.Y. That said couple having formally and legally agreed to separate, dissolve and cease matrimonial relations, now pray we the court that said property, one wooden boat of sailing type, known as an Abeking-Rassmussen Yawl of German origin and marketed in this country, the United States of America, by one Concordia Boat Company of Padanarum, Massachusetts. That said boat named the 'The Gentle Spirit' be immediately seized and placed at Public Auction, the proceeds of which be placed in trust for the education of the couple's children: Timothy James age (6), Samantha Anne age (5) and Jonathan Samuel age (3). Said auction to be held immediately within the week to prevent Mr. O'Keefe from absconding with said property as he is wont to do from past experience..."

"Objection, your honor!"

"Shut up and sit down!"

"Your honor, there are already college funds established for the children. This petition is redundant and punitive..."

"Shut up, Mr. Goldstein and sit down or I'll find you in contempt." The judge was banging his gavel.

I was in a cold rage. They had literally stripped me of everything and now she wanted to take away my sailboat, the only real enjoyment I ever got out of life and the bitch knew it. I stood very slowly, pushed back my chair, walked around the table and started toward the judge. They came at me from both sides, one on the left with his nightstick drawn, the one on the right reaching for his gun.

These were the court's bailiffs, as they were called, glorified errand boys, nothing more than ushers, someone's relatives appointed to a patronage job. They were too eager to prove themselves. Amateurs! I palmed the left one in the chin and heard his neck snap. The one on the right never cleared his holster with his gun. I clobbered him in the head with a reverse kick. It should have been over right then but Selma Freidman, Natalie's attorney, decided to prove how macho she was. She hated men and she was determined to finish me off once and for all before I got out of that courtroom. She came screaming at me with a sharpened number two Eagle pencil raised over her head. She was no amateur. She was a competent, well trained, highly motivated "man killer". I caught her arm on the downswing, twisted down and away while hip checking the bitch and dumping her as hard as I dared on the floor. It was effective. I broke her wrist and knocked her out cold. So there I stood, bodies all around me, hysteria in all corners of the courtroom. The judge stood up and stared at the scene before him.

"You've destroyed my courtroom, you goddamned animal." He waved his gavel at me like a stubby rapier, as if to fend me off.

"Shut up and sit down, you maggot. I've got something I want to say to you." He sat. "You people are scum," I continued. "You steal from a man but no one arrests you or puts you in jail because you hide behind the law. You think it's a joke to take a man's life and tear it apart and help the vultures pick his bones. Well, ENOUGH ALREADY GODDAMN YOU! That boat is mine. It's in my name. It's all I've got left and nobody, do you understand me, NOBODY, is going to take it away from me. If you try, you'll never see that boat or me ever again. I'm the only one who knows where it is and if you try to take it, I'll go get on it and I'll point it south and you'll never see me or one lousy penny ever again. Do you understand me, you little maggot?" The judge nodded his head. There were policemen filing into the courtroom now. They were real and they were pros. No amateurs. The only way past them would be to kill each one. Not a good way to go but I no longer cared. I'd been totally betrayed by the very system for which I'd fought and risked my life.

"Call your dogs off, judge, or there's going to be a real blood bath right here and now. This is what I'm trained for. It's what I lived for in Vietnam. I don't care how it ends."

Saul Goldstein intervened at that point and it's probably the only reason I'm still alive. He stood up like nothing had happened and made a motion just as if court was still in session. He was probably correct in what he did because everyone acted like it was the next thing on the agenda and it restored order to the courtroom.

"Your honor, defense moves for a brief recess." There was instant silence. All eyes and ears were turned toward the judge. He pounded his gavel, stood and pointed at the bodies on the floor.

"Granted. Clean up this mess. Mr. Goldstein, Mr. O'Keefe and Mrs. O'Keefe...in my chambers, NOW!"

We gathered in the judge's chambers. No one made a move to sit down. Even Judge Larry Gould remained standing.

"I want to ask Mr. O'Keefe something."

"What is it, your Honor?"

"What sort of deal will you accept right here and now?"

"Your honor, I don't think Mr. O'Keefe is in any condition right now..." Saul intervened.

"Shut up, Saul! Let Mr. O'Keefe decide." His hands were shaking. That's what happens to intellectuals who are not accustomed to violence. They participate in all sorts of conspiracies and power plays to control others but when they squeeze someone too tightly and things get out of hand, they can't take it. They aren't able to accept the fact that life isn't an intellectual pursuit. Judge Gould was realistic enough to know he had to deal temporarily outside accepted legal procedure.

"I don't mind supporting my family, Judge. I'll take the boat, the cottage and the Caddy. She can have the rest. Give me joint custody and call it a deal."

The judge turned to Natalie. "Mrs. O'Keefe?"

"That's not fair. I don't want him near my children. You've seen what he's like. He's a monster."

"Has he ever hurt you, Mrs. O'Keefe?"

"Why...Ahh...No! But..."

"Be quiet, woman!" Judge Giles turned to Saul Goldstein.

"Saul?"

"O.K. with me your honor if it's all right with Bill."

"Right. That settles that. Now I have the problem of the attacks on my staff and the plaintiff's attorney. I've never seen such efficient destructive force in all my life, Mr. O'Keefe. You are obviously a professional. I can charge you with every sort of crime in the book and if one of those people dies, I will."

"They started it, your honor. When someone comes at me like that with lethal weapons, I don't stop to think."

"You may have a problem here, Judge, especially if the press gets hold of what was going on." Saul had a twinkle in his eyes. I decided to let him handle it.

"The press is not going to get hold of anything, Saul."

"They will if you charge my client, Larry."

"Point taken. Let's drop it. We'll call a truce and everyone will remain as they are."

"Done!" said Saul.

So I got the Cadillac Eldorado Coupe, sailboat, summer cottage and my freedom. For a while I would come to the cottage and all the painful memories of the divorce would come flooding back so I'd leave. Then I started changing things until it was home. I insulated the whole building: attic, walls, crawl space, put in new windows, built a foundation and put in new wood stoves. I installed a gravity feed water system and a solar heated panel for hot water. I put in a specially designed holding tank to satisfy the Nature Conservancy people.

The house is a cape style building set back about three hundred yards from the water overlooking a wildlife refuge in the dunes. It was there before the refuge was established and remained with certain restrictions: no septic systems, wells, telephone poles, asphalt driveways, flag poles, TV antennas, docks, boathouses, coal burning stoves or furnaces and more. It's a quiet refuge from a world of deception and violence. It suits my life and work. When I'm there, I'm beyond the reach of the telephone and the life where people lie, cheat, steal and hurt each other. Now, whenever I come home, I don't feel the overwhelming emotions from the brutalizing divorce. It's my home and I spend time here whenever I'm not working.

Willie Monk used to come visit me when he was free and we would fish, sail and walk the beach, comparing notes and sharing ideas until he had a stroke about a year ago. We were walking the beach, picking up shells when he just fell down. I carried him to the cottage and went for help. His ex-wife put him in a nursing home, a fate worse than death for a man like Willie who was accustomed to an active and independent life.

I've had Willie out to the cottage several times since his stroke. Each time I have to secure written permission from his family, which they never grant without some sort of hassle: just their way of maintaining control. I would bring him out, help him walk, dragging one dead leg behind him, to the front porch where he could sit and watch the water, the boats, the birds and the clouds go by. There he would sit for hours, unable to speak, incapacitated, incapable of smiling or talking and only occasionally moving his head to follow something that caught his interest. I thought it was all a waste of time the first few visits until it was time for him to go back to the nursing home. When I came to take him from his porch chair, he would start to cry.

Now, I was home again and I needed time to heal. My left arm and shoulder were beginning to hurt as the shot and pills wore off. I was tired, discouraged and maybe even a little depressed. Something was rotten in East Harbour: Harry Dondi had folded under pressure. That was not like him. Connie Wilson was a beautiful woman beyond my reach. Willie Monk was gone but not forgotten, and I got the worst of it the past few days. Oh well, it was over and Harry had what he needed to stop the payment on the claim. So what now, O'Keefe? The answer came from deep down inside my psyche. "Forget it. You gave it your best shot for now. Just let it go and keep on moving."

The sun was setting in the western sky with the tide on the ebb. The summer sea breeze from the southwest would soon die and turn to a land breeze as things cooled off. I poured a couple fingers of Isly Single Malt Scotch Whiskey neat, popped four aspirin, sat on the front porch of the cottage in Willie Monk's chair and watched the sun go down. What more could a man ask? ✳

CHAPTER NINE

Morning comes early on the dunes. Salt air and nature's changing elements give a man a unique feeling of vigor and renewal. Anyone who lives near the ocean has experienced its intense energy and vitality. I'm usually awake at sunrise, but today the sun was climbing high in the morning sky and I was still wrapped in a deep slumber when a noise woke me. It took a few moments to realize where I was, then I tried to sit up and it all came back in a wave of pain. I staggered from the bedroom to the door to find Dr. John Smith on the front porch, black bag in hand, professional smile on his face.

"Good morning, Mr. O'Keefe. I'm headed back to the city today. Thought I'd check in to see how you're doing."

"How'd you find me, Doc? Just happen to be in the neighborhood?"

"Harry told me to keep you in good shape in case he has to call you back." He indicated a chair and I sat down.

"Not likely, Doc. Harry knows the rules." He took his stethoscope out of his bag.

"Yes, we all know the rules but you don't seem to follow them. Harry says you're very good but so far all you've done is scare hell out of everyone in East Harbour and State Mutual Insurance." He thumped my back and listened. "One of those men you beat up is still in a coma. If he dies, you'll be charged with murder. How does that make you feel?"

"I don't think about those things. They did the attacking. They're the criminals. It's simple."

"No remorse, heh?"

"People who engage in violence should be ready to accept the consequences. They never picture themselves as victims. This isn't child's play. Tell me, John, what's your real name? Couldn't you and Harry find a better cover name than Smith?"

"I know you guys use pseudonyms when you're doing this sort of work but that is my real name. I'm a doctor of internal medicine at the Manhattan West Clinic for Women. Not one of your insurance doctor types." He laughed.

"Then how did you ever get into this deal with Harry?"

"I married Nicki, his oldest daughter. We were on vacation at my family's home on the point with the two children when Harry called me for help. I never dreamed it was something like this. I could lose my license to practice. But if I can't help a man who's been injured, why did I become a doctor?"

"So, you're Harry's son-in-law? Did he sell you life insurance?"

"How'd you know? That's actually how we met. He came to City Hospital when I was interning and gave a seminar on how to cut insurance costs by spotting fraudulent claims. We already knew most of it but after the seminar, Harry put the bite on us to sign up for some universal life policy. He had his wife, Joannie, and Nicki pass out brochures. I fell in love and bought a policy." He removed the dressing.

"Yeh, good old Harry. He'd sell his own mother if she was still alive. We go back aways in the insurance business."

"He told me about it. He has a great deal of respect for you and he's very disappointed that you left him on the East Harbour thing. He asked me to tell you that he understands.

"So, are you here as Harry's personal envoy?"

"I should be offended by that remark." He ripped off the last piece of gauze. It was stuck to the wound by dried blood and it hurt. "But I'm going to make allowances for the two of you. Harry told me about you and Willie Monk, your divorce and some of the cases you solved. He says you and Willie made history, especially on that Chicago factory fire case where you proved the body wasn't the owner and then traced him down alive in Aruba, kidnapped him and brought him back to stand trial. He says you're the best in the business anywhere."

"Gee whiz, Doc. Stop it already. You're giving me a swelled head." He squeezed my left arm and pulled at a couple of the stitches. It hurt but not like before.

"It's healing well. How's it feel?"

"Better. Before, I thought I was dead. Now I just wish I was."

"Always joking, huh, O'Keefe? Everything's funny in your world."

"That's right. Everything's funny. Just depends how you sit on it."

"Yes, of course." He laughed and started dressing the wound again. "Keep this dry. It should be all right but don't take any chances. I'll leave you some antibiotics. Make sure you take them. There's nothing worse than surviving a bad cut like this and then dying of an infection."

"You're wrong, Doc."

"How's that, O'Keefe?"

"There's nothing worse in life than living with ignorance."

"Point well taken, but please do as I say. There's more at stake here than just your arm." He stuck a needle into a bottle and filled a syringe.

"How's that feel.?" He stuck the needle in my good arm.

"Feels great when it stops hurting." He pulled it out.

"You told Harry the way to crack this Murry Berman thing. Well, you were probably right. Did you bother to read the files on Murry's death before you got jumped?" I nodded. "Yes, well, did you notice the date of death and the date of notification to the insurance company?"

"Yes, everything was within parameters. Death occurred August 1st and notification was August 5th. Payment of the claim must be made within thirty days after the day of notification, exclusive of holidays, which would make it this coming Wednesday since Monday is Labor Day. The law is very explicit. Notification of death with a proper death certificate within thirty days and payment or letter contesting payment within thirty days to the beneficiary after the date of notification. Look! What's the big deal? Harry has all he needs to stop the payment of that claim. I gave it to him. State Mutual did $67 billion in face value whole life insurance sales last year. They declared a dividend to their investors, that's the policy-holders, of $77.5 mil on a gross profit of $335 million. That's a 2.3% return on investment for the poor dumb schmucks who were stupid enough to buy that sort of insurance."

"I'm one of those poor dumb schumcks, Bill."

"Right, and if you could count, Doc, you'd take that insurance policy, stuff it in Harry's left ear, and never pay another penny for a whole life or universal life or any other sort of nifty, so-called, savings and investment plan type life insurance because it's an outright rip off. Do you think paying me 10% of six million is going to hurt State Mutual? Hell, they could easily pay the whole amount to Lydia Berman and never even skip a heartbeat. There's a reason guys like me make what we do. It's the principle of the thing. Insurance companies don't like to look like a soft touch so they have hired guns like me to scare people who even think about defrauding them. Meanwhile, the insurance company is defrauding the living hell out of everybody: the customer, their employees, the public, the state, the nation, you name it."

"Aren't you being just a bit hard on State Mutual and insurance companies in general? After all, we do need them, and you've made a good living off them, haven't you?"

"Yes, and they've made a damn good living off me, too. In just one year alone, Willie Monk and I saved State Mutual over ninety million in claims, and there wasn't a single case of fraud in the bunch, just old ladies and sick old men, who didn't sign on the right line, or forgot to pay their premiums or couldn't afford a lawyer. Willie and I made less than $50,000 each that year. Do you think John Stanley, the president of State Mutual, cares about Murry Berman or his wife and kids? Hell no, Doctor! He just wants to show me who's boss. So I work for 10% or I don't work, and believe me, that'll get around. John won't get anybody to work for him again."

"They're going to fire Harry if he doesn't solve the case. Harry's in East Harbour right now looking for clues about how Murry Berman died. If he doesn't find something, they'll fire him. I'll end up supporting him."

"That would be the best thing ever happened. Joannie would love it and she'd keep Harry so busy he'd never have to worry about anything. After awhile he'd adjust and never miss State Mutual. Shit! Listen to me. Tell Harry to stay out of East Harbour. It's no place for an amateur."

"But Harry has to solve this case. John Stanley told him to, and Harry really isn't an amateur you know."

"Look damn it! The case is solved as far as insurance fraud is concerned. Harry had it in his files all the time. He just didn't know what to look for and that makes him an amateur. All Harry has to do is clear it with the legal department and notify the grieving widow there's no payment, and he's a hero."

"But then you don't get paid anything, O'Keefe. Harry said you even turned down the $25,000. Are you crazy?"

"You don't get it, Doc. Harry isn't just a friend. He's a buddy. We don't rat on a buddy. We don't lie to a buddy. We don't let a buddy go point alone and we always cover a buddy's backside. Harry covered for me yesterday when I was leaving East Harbour, and it's a good thing he did or I'd probably be in jail right now."

"He told me about that but why would you be in jail? Myron Gates didn't have anything on you. He had no reason to cause you any trouble."

"That's just the point, Doc. He stopped me because he was afraid to let me leave town alive. I knew that, so did Harry. If I got out of my car, one of us would have died. Harry showed up, and Myron couldn't do his dirty work because there was a witness."

"So what makes you think you would have been successful in getting the better of Myron Gates. Maybe he would have killed you."

"I never go into a fight with the slightest doubt about the outcome. I believe I can win or I don't fight, and I'm always prepared to accept the consequences."

"Sounds like a really brutal way to live."

"No, Doc. It's not brutal, it's just reality and maybe you should start looking at it that way. It's called life and it can be very brutal and violent. It's up to those of us who live it to make our choices. Some run away and hide. Some pretend it's something it isn't, and some of us participate when necessary and then we get out."

"You're in the last category, I take it?"

"Yes. I'm not always proud of what I've done, but I can say that I've always been honest with my friends and they've always been honest with me."

"So honesty is very important? Unfortunately, it's not always accepted in this world."

"Very true. Look. Tell Harry to get out of East Harbour. It's not safe there. The State Department of Insurance, State Police, even the F.B.I. can handle it. Tell him he doesn't need to be there."

"I will and you keep that arm dry and quiet. By the way, here are the computer runs you asked for. I'll leave them here on the table.

I stood on the side porch and watched him go. He waved before getting into his car. I liked Doctor John Smith. He still had just the right amount of idealism. With luck, he wouldn't have to give that up the way some of us have. I gave the beach a cursory glance, noticed the tide was out and remembered I hadn't seen my sailboat in two days. I'd eaten chicken noodle soup at Connie Wilson's. "Time to eat and check out the sailboat, O'Keefe," I said. "Sounds good to me," I answered.

The eastern end of Long Island tends to isolation with sections of long sandy beaches, stunted pine and oak strewn dunes. Proposals were made to build bridges to the mainland but the cost and engineering problems were too great. Congestion on the Long Island Expressway gets worse every year. The expressway ends before the Great Peconic Bay and smaller roads extend beyond to the end of the island. The area is characterized by a number of bays and islands which make it a sailor's paradise, and if that isn't enough, there's always Long Island Sound, Block Island Sound and open ocean sailing, definitely not for the faint-hearted when stormy weather strikes.

My sailboat at Green's Marina is across from Sag Harbor, inside the two most eastern points of Long Island, Orient Point and Montauk Point. This gives me access to some of the best sailing waters in the world. I stopped at Gabby's Diner for lunch and continued out to the marina. All was well and as I stepped on board the boat, my body went through a change. It's difficult to explain. The heartbeat of a sailor is different from that of a landsman. I guess you just have to experience it.

I opened the hatches to let her air out and began straightening up. I coiled and stowed lines, bumpers and life jackets. The binnacle compass wasn't covered. I made a mental note to speak to Timmy. A chart case needed tidying up under the port seat in the cockpit, the brass wheel cover was ripped, a frayed line, a patch of peeling varnish on the cabin sole bright work and so it went for most of the afternoon. Friends came by and chatted, some offered advice, others offered to help, but those who knew me just chatted.

At one point about midway in the afternoon, Timmy dropped off the mail. I tossed the bundle down onto the chart table and around sundown I began to feel better about the shape the boat was in, so I stopped to have a beer and watch the Sunday evening activity in the marina. Boats were coming into the docks to unload before going out to their moorings. Those that had slips were maneuvering into them, each one using a different set of procedures, trying to make a smooth docking without any embarrassing moments, or worse yet, damage to boat or docks.

One family always had trouble docking and invariably provided a few moments of entertainment for the whole marina. Anthony Vitalli made his money in the concrete business and the one thing he wanted more than love itself, was a boat, not just any boat but a powerboat, you know, "The biggest freekin' motorboat on the block." That's the way Anthony saw things, so the biggest was the best and that's what he wanted. Obviously, when you're accustomed to navigating a big old cement truck around all day, a big old motorboat is no problem, right? "After all, what's the difference between a truck and a boat? They both got wheels, right?" So, Tony went out and bought the first big boat he liked at the New York Boat Show, a 52′ Chesapeake Bay cabin cruiser with twin Chrysler 457's; three cabins: captain's, main salon, and guest, hot and cold pressurized water, two heads with showers, combo electric/gas refrigerator, lights, heat and air, ship to shore, LORAN, GPS, radar and interlinking automatic copilots for main and flying bridge, steering systems with interlocks, etc. No expense was spared in getting the boat ready for sea that first spring. Tina Vitalli decorated the interior with red velvet curtains and expensive deep pile red carpeting to match.

On the first sail they took the six kids, ages 3, 5, 6, 8,10, and 12, plus Mama and Papa Vitalli, three or four aunts and uncles, a brother or two with wives and kids, and a neighbor. They piled aboard Saturday morning, and took off for a day on the water, narrowly missing the main dock and half the boats in the harbor. Everyone in the marina chipped into a pool, betting on when they would be back. I took 2:00 P.M. because I figured with that crowd, they would stay out until the food ran out and then come back. I lost. Tony ran the engines at full throttle till they overheated and seized up, leaving the whole boatload rocking and rolling around until the Coast Guard arrived to tow them in.

They ran out of food long before help arrived and after several hours of rolling around, half the adults and all the kids were sea sick, the decks were awash with soiled clothing, beer cans, broken pretzels and potato chips. It was 6:00 P.M. when they arrived in tow at Green's Marina. The Coast Guard cutter was commanded by a Lieutenant Giorski, who lacked a sense of humor and proved it by citing Tony for not having any fire extinguishers or life jackets on board the badly overloaded boat. He further warned Tony that if he ever saw him out on the water again, he would automatically pull him over and give him and his boat the toughest inspection the law would allow. The Lieutenant needn't have worried, however, because it took Tony the rest of the season to fix the engines. They didn't rid the vessel of the smell of the voyage until the carpets and curtains were ripped out and replaced with more sensible indoor/outdoor carpets and washable cotton curtains.

That was two years ago. Tony and Tina used their off-season time to attend the Coast Guard Auxiliary courses and they joined the Shelter Island Power Squadron. He limits the number of guests on board at any one time and all the kids wear life vests from the time they leave dry land until they return. In spite of all these efforts at improvement, Tony and Tina with their 52' cruiser, remain the center of attention and the butt of a few indelicate comments every time they ship in or out. Like now. I spotted the huge bulk of the Concrete Maiden rounding the point coming up channel, Tony on the flying bridge, picking his way carefully around the buoys and sand bars, yelling orders to everyone on the boat. Even at that distance, his booming voice carried across the water, loud and clear.

"Tina! Get that kid off the transom."

"Anthony," Tony's eldest, now a strapping fifteen, "man the bow line and don't fall overboard."

"Mimi! Run and get the bumpers. Quick now!"

"Tina, for crying out loud, get that kid off the transom before he falls over!"

"Get 'em yourself, stupid! I got a fire in the galley."

"Oh shit!"

So it went until they reached the marina's main dock where Tony neatly tucked his 52' baby up to the gas docks. "Little" Tony jumped onto the floating platform and deftly secured his ¾" nylon line to an oversized cleat with two twists of the wrist, trotted aft to do the same with the stern line handed to him by the kid, his brother on the transom, while Mimi ran up and down the deck adjusting the lines on the bumpers to keep the topsides from being scratched. Meanwhile, Captain Tony shut down his twin Chrysler 457's, his babies he calls them, all the while continuing the torrent of commands and instructions to his crew. Tina emerges from the main salon, face blackened, fire extinguisher in hand, looks around and yells, "Nice job, gang," and disappears below amid a puff of smoke. ❋

CHAPTER TEN

The sun was setting in an orange-yellow haze to the west. A cool breeze off the ocean, wafted in with the incoming tide while a pair of cormorants skimmed the azure water still searching for schools of fish near the surface. The Vitalli clan was long gone back to their suburban north Jersey home for another week in the tread-mill and the marina dock lights were blinking on. I was feeling pretty mellow and life was looking all right after a day of tinkering. Marty and Grace Gomes, two slips down the dock, invited me aboard for cocktails, hors d'oeurves and, as I found out when I arrived, a chance to meet Marty Gomes' sister, Ginger. Ah yes, life can be very good and Ginger Gomes, all 5'8" of her was a most beautiful young lady, stewardess for Trans Air, based in San Diego. 'Perhaps Mr. O'Keefe would like some help tomorrow sailing his yawl? Just so happens Ginger has a few days off and since tomorrow is Monday and Marty and the little lady have to go back to the big city to earn more bread to pay for their expensive lifestyle, it seems there won't be anyone to watch after little ole' Ginger...hint, hint, hint'. What could I say? We agreed to sail on the morning tide at 8:30 A.M. sharp and I returned to my boat to spend the night in celibate contemplation.

The mail waited on the chart table so I picked it up and idly thumbed through it as I walked into the main cabin. I scratched a match, lit the gimbaled lamp and sat on the starboard bunk, propping my back up with a couple of pillows and continued sorting. There was the usual junk: flyers, advertising inserts, special offers addressed to occupant and a free trip to Florida to look at the condo I'd just won. There were magazines, a letter from Natalie and the kids and about a dozen messages from Harry Dondi, all saying the same thing, "Call immediately". The investigator in me kicked in and I sorted the messages by date and time, checking the telephone numbers at the bottom of each to trace Harry's movements. The first came from his office in Manhattan, early that morning. The next two had the same number indicating that he stayed there until 10:35 A.M. The next three messages were from his home. I recognized the number. Then he must have gone straight to East Harbour where he contacted Connie Wilson. Her private number was on the next six messages, each one showing more anxiety than the one before. They went from, "please call", to, "call immediately"; to "I gotta talk to you now!" It was after 10:00 P.M. but I knew I'd never sleep unless I talked to him so I walked up to the pay phone outside the marina office and dialed Connie's number, using my telephone credit card. She answered on the third ring, sounding sleepy and a little irritable.

"Hello!"

"Hello yourself, lady."

"Bill! It's about time you called. Where the hell are you?"

"I'm at Green's Marina. Just got Harry's messages. Is he there?"

"Oh, Bill! I don't know where he is. He's been in and out of here since this afternoon. Doctor Smith stopped in. Harry was more upset after he left. He paced around here for almost an hour reading those reports, muttering to himself how he was so blind and stupid and you were right. Then he left."

"Where did he go?"

"I don't know. He mentioned cleaning up this mess. Then he said thanks and if you called, to say he owed you. Bill, I'm really afraid."

"There's no need to be afraid. Stay in your apartment. Stay clear of Myron Gates. After Harry stops payment the whole thing will be out in the open and no one will get hurt."

"But what about all the things they did? Murry Berman must have been murdered for that insurance policy and other people are involved. Something needs to be done to catch everybody and put them in jail. John Stanley told Harry that if he couldn't prove Murry Berman was really murdered, he'd fire Harry and anyone else involved."

"That's not our job. It will be enough if Harry can stop the payment of that six million dollar claim on a technicality. The state's criminal investigative team can handle the rest. The Attorney General and the State Police have all the resources to handle any further investigation. This is their sort of party. Our job is only to stop the payment of the life insurance claim. Let the pros do the rest. They're better at it. Harry knows that. He shouldn't be messing around out there. As for John Stanley, he's just blowing smoke to make himself look good."

"You make it sound so simple, Bill. I wish I could have as much confidence in what you say as you do."

"It's not all that complicated, Babe. Just be careful and lay low. When the payoff is stopped, they won't have any motive to hurt anyone. After Wednesday they'll run for cover, so just take it easy and wait them out. I'm going sailing tomorrow and I'll call you when I get back in…that is, if you want me to?"

"I'd like you to call me. Will I see you again, Bill?"

"You can count on it. Just take care of yourself, Connie."

"You too, O'Keefe. Goodbye."

I had an uneasy feeling in my gut as I walked back to my boat and it had nothing to do with guilt. Maybe I was stringing Connie along just a little but going slow had its merits. Besides, she might have someone else tucked away in her private hotel hideaway or even back in Iowa. No! The funny feeling in my gut wasn't guilt about Connie Wilson. It was a premonition that Harry Dondi was in deep trouble and didn't have the brains to know it. I had a compulsive urge to rush back to East Harbour to save my friend and then sleep with the little lady, but I knew better. That's the problem when you become a pro and lose your innocence in the gristmills of life. My high school history teacher taught me that people and civilizations proceed on an upward curve, always producing bigger, better and more satisfying results. My mother said things always turn out all right, but Vietnam taught me a different sense of history. Things don't always work out for the best. People and civilizations don't follow an upscale curve and life isn't perfect.

I opened the letter from Natalie before going to sleep; another mistake. It consisted mainly of complaints and accusations about her lifestyle, the children, the neighbors and the general condition of things as I'd left them. She was an unhappy woman and everything she touched became tarnished with unhappiness. I would have to make an effort very soon to get the children a more positive living arrangement. Timothy, (11), needed a man's point of view in his life. Samantha, (10), would turn into a carbon copy of her mother, no matter what I did to prevent it. She already hated me for all the mean things I did to her helpless mother. Little Jonathan (8) was a happy-go-lucky kid, who still had time. 'Go to sleep, O'Keefe. Forget it and get on with your life.' I fell asleep to the gurgling of water lapping against the hull, just inches from my brain. Sometime during the night, the gimbaled lamp burned out and the darkness was complete.

"Hello? Yoo Hoo, Hello? Time to rise and shine." Ginger stood over me, smiling from ear to ear, shaking my bad shoulder. I came fully awake as the pain shot through my body.

"Ahh...ouch! Okay...Okay, I'm up. You can stop now." I rolled to a sitting position and banged my head on the overhead bunk. Ginger stood there, a true vision of beauty, glowing with enthusiasm. Her pink shorts were too short revealing plenty of detail, and the tank top was too small for her ample bosom. Short blond hair brushed her shoulders and the flush of excitement showed through her tanned complexion. She was more woman than I remembered from last night. Not small and all in the right places.

"What time is it?" I tried standing up but the muscles in my back and left shoulder screamed in pain.

"It's daylight, almost 6:00 A.M., Bill. Marty and Grace left an hour ago. I'm so excited I couldn't wait any longer. Marty told me how important it is to catch the tide with a sailboat and how it slows you down if you try to sail against the tide. What a beautiful metaphor, 'sailing against the tide'. Now I'll get a chance to see what it really means...Oh my! Are you all right?" She was looking at my arm. Blood had leaked through my bandage and shirt.

"Sure, just a little scratch. Feeling better now." I walked unsteadily to the galley, forward of the main cabin, stubbing my toe on a bulkhead.

"Had your breakfast yet?"

I lit the stove and put the kettle on. The first step in any successful voyage is to make the coffee. After a sailboat is under way, it's virtually impossible to even think about lighting a stove. I dropped the main salon table and set silverware, napkins, cups and saucers.

"Where would you like to go today, Ginger?"

"Oh! I was talking to Marty and Grace and they said we should go to Block Island. Grace says it's fun, that we can go hiking and see the whole island on a bicycle in one day. Can we do that?"

"We'll see how the winds are. If they're blowing the right direction and the tides are favorable, maybe we can go to Block Island. It's at least forty miles, which could take most of the day. How much time do you have?"

"No problem. I don't have to be in San Diego until Thursday, so I can spend at least three days with you...that is, if you can stand having me around?" She looked at me. "Sometimes I get on people's nerves. I just hope that doesn't happen with us. Grace said not to worry, that you were a special kind of man and you would understand me."

"We'll get along just fine, Ginger. Sailing is a sport where a person can become totally involved, mentally, physically and emotionally. People become passionately addicted to it for life."

"I just hope I do everything the right way. I don't want to make any mistakes. People say I have a confidence problem. That's why I talk so much. What do you think?"

"I think you'll enjoy this more than anything you've ever done. It'll boost your self-confidence. So just relax and let it all hang out. When this is over, you'll be Captain of the ship." She seemed relieved.

We finished a light breakfast of coffee and English muffins with chutney. I went to the office and picked up a 50# block of ice, a case of coke and some groceries for a couple of days on the water. I filled the water tanks, fueled up, started the engine, charged the batteries, removed the sail covers, stowed anything loose, checked the weather, especially the long range forecast and cast off at 9:00 A.M. sharp on an outgoing tide. The winds were fluky inside so I motored until we were around the point of Ram Island, then I headed it up into a southwesterly of about ten knots and raised the mainsail. It went up without a hitch and so did the jib, but the mizzen jammed three quarters of the way up and I had to pull it down and reset it several times before I found the problem. Ginger was standing on the line. We got that straightened out in a hurry. I showed her how to hold the bow into the wind while I raised the sails, but she got confused so I sailed with everything set loose for a couple of hours. Around the lee shore of Gardiners Island I reset the sails and tightened everything up before we hit the open seas. We took turns at the wheel and the rest of the day was a very pleasant sail to Block Island where we found a mooring in the Great Salt Pond by 5:00 P.M. Not bad for a couple of amateurs, hey what? We furled the sails, cleaned her up, washed down the decks and rowed ashore in the dingy for a quick look at the town before dark. After a bite to eat at the Salty Dog Pub, we made our way back to the boat in the dark, both of us slightly tipsy from the wine we'd shared at dinner. We spent the rest of the evening in the main salon with the lamp lit and a couple of fingers of good Scotch whiskey all 'round.

"O'Keefe. This is, without a doubt, the most fun I've ever had. It even beats flying." She'd loosened up considerably. She looked at me, moved closer and planted a big juicy kiss square on my lips.

"Hope you don't mind."

"Not at all."

It was quick and urgent. As we lay there holding each other, I wondered if Ginger had much experience with men.

"I'm sorry if I didn't last long, Bill, but I guess I don't have much experience with this sort of thing. I really appreciate you being so understanding with me." The old confidence problem.

"You have nothing to apologize for...I guess I haven't had much experience with this sort of thing either".

Most people assume that a single man just naturally gets lots of action in his life. Well, I'm here to tell you, it ain't necessarily so. We have this image of the hard boiled private investigator, running around, using and losing voluptuous women all over the landscape. Such is the stuff of fiction. Since my divorce, I'd buried myself in work. Romance was a now-and-then thing but seldom a real part of my life. Then there was the problem of my work and the dark side of my past, which occasionally surfaced, like in the courtroom, that day, five years ago. Few women can live with a man who has the capability of destroying life at the drop of a hat. So, living alone was my best option.

We were tired and fell asleep right there. We slept soundly for quite awhile with our own dreams and then sometime in the night, we made love again, less urgently, more meaningfully, exploring the depths and heights of each other's bodies and emotions. Then, we slept more soundly than before.

Suddenly, there was banging and shouting, bright lights and the boat was rocking. Someone had come aboard in the night and was shining a light down the main hatch.

"Hey! Anybody there? Ahoy there aboard the Gentle Spirit? Are you there, damn it?"

"Yo! What do you want?" We untangled ourselves from the awkward position we were in.

"Harbor Master here. I got a message for you. Come on deck."

"Be right there." I reached above the bunk and took my .44 Magnum out of its holster, slipped on a pair of shorts, staggered in the dark to the ladder, cocked the gun and looked up through the main hatch.

"You Captain O'Keefe of the Gentle Spirit?"

"Show your face." He did and I recognized him as the Harbor Master, Jake Mattos. "What do you want?"

"I got a message for you, Captain. They said it was an emergency and to have you call Green's Marina on Long Island right away. I got the number right here." I flipped on the chart table light and took the slip of paper he handed down to me.

"My batteries are down. I'll have to start the engine." I climbed the ladder into the cockpit, turned on the bilge fan and waited about thirty seconds, then turned the ignition key to start the glow plugs, waited fifteen seconds and hit the starter button. The engine started right up. I let it warm up at 1000 RPM.

"The weather's shifting. What's going on?"

"Frontal passage. Maybe a quick nor'easter. Either way we're in for some fun with all the summer sailors rollin' around out there in their little tubs." A boy in a tender alongside was standing up, holding on to a line like a true sailor, no other support.

"Sounds like you don't have much use for us tourists, Jake."

"Oh, you're not like them others, Captain. I watched you bring her in. You're no tourist, Captain O'Keefe. You're a sailor. Yeh, and they told me to watch out and not try to sneak up on you so I made plenty of noise coming aboard. Looks like they was right." He pointed to my gun.

"Sorry, just a reflex action and thanks for the compliment. I appreciate it, coming from you." I increased the power to 1500 RPM and went below, turned on the radio, switched the channel and waited for it to stabilize.

"Point Judith Marine ... Point Judith Marine ... this is the sailing yacht Gentle Spirit, over?"

"Sailing yacht Gentle Spirit, Point Judith Marine, I read you five by, go ahead, over." A woman's voice answered. Good old Coast Guard.

"Point Judith, sailing yacht Gentle Spirit, request you place a collect call to Green's Marina, Long Island ..." I gave her the number.

"Roger, Gentle Spirit, standby one." I waited. The harbormaster was still standing in the cockpit. Ginger had managed to put on some clothes. I was aware of a drop in temperature and wondered how bad it would be.

"Sailing yacht, Gentle Spirit, your party is on the line. Go ahead, over."

"Hello. This is O'Keefe, over."

"Hello, Bill, this is Tom Green. We've been waiting for your call. I've got some bad news for you, over."

"I'm in Block Island, the weather's going down, and I'm out of beer. What could be worse, Tom, over?" I could hear him laughing.

"Okay, Bill, I read you, but this is serious. Your friend, Harry Dondi, was found late tonight, shot several times and left for dead in a ditch along the highway in East Harbour. He's in County Hospital, critical condition, unconscious. I don't know much else, over." It hit me between the eyes. For a moment I just stood there, dumbfounded.

"I ... understand ... Tom. I don't know what to say. I'm stuck here in Block Island and the weather is turning sour. I can't possibly get out of here before morning so I probably won't be much help until tomorrow evening, over."

"That sounds about right, Bill, but maybe you could leave the boat there and fly over to the mainland in the morning, over." Jake, gestured to me.

"Stand by one, Tom ..."

"I can get you out of here in the dark, Captain. I know the channel if you'll trust me. There ain't no airplanes till noon." I gave him the thumbs up.

"Tom, I've got a pilot, so I should be out of here within the hour. With luck, we should make it by mid morning, over."

"Right, sounds good. Be careful friend. We'll be standing by, over."

I turned to Ginger, "You may not want to do this one, Babe. It's going to be rough and just a bit dangerous."

"I'll stick with you, O'Keefe. I think I've regained my confidence." She gave me a kiss on the cheek. "Just do us all a favor, will you, and put that cannon away. You're scaring everyone." I was still holding the .44 Magnum. I put it on the chart table.

"Captain? My boy, Danny, is in my tender. He's an able sailor. You might take him along for insurance. He would have gone to the Maritime Academy but we didn't have the money. He won't be a burden."

"I can use the help. I'll pay whatever it's worth for his time."

"No need o' that, Captain. Sounds like you'll be needing all the help God can give you."

He was right. It was one thing to take a leisurely sail on a sunny afternoon with a ten knot breeze but night sailing with a nor'easter on your back side in strange waters with an inexperienced crew is nothing but pure insanity. Was I justified in taking such a risk or was I just being melodramatic? If Harry Dondi ignored my advice, it was his own fault or was I showing off for Connie Wilson, 'White Knight' O'Keefe to the rescue? No, damn it! East Harbour was a pigsty and I'd never be able to live with myself if I let it ride any longer. It was time to put a stop to the fun and games and I knew how to do it.

We picked our way, under power, out of the Great Salt Pond, into the channel and out into the open ocean. Jake was all business once we were under way. He didn't say much, just pointed or nodded to indicate the lights or landmarks by which he was navigating. Once clear of the narrow gut, with its rocky sea walls, he stayed at the wheel, swung the bow to a westerly heading and pointed his finger at the binnacle compass, now back lighted in red. The heading was 295 degrees.

"Take you to the bell and home." He turned to Danny and gestured to the tender trailing behind us. Danny grabbed the line and pulled the tender alongside.

"Your mamma'll have dinner ready when you get back." Then, without any further ceremony, Jake hopped over the side into the tender like a man half his age, started the engine, waved and disappeared into the night. Men of the sea; no sentiment, no emotion, no warnings to be careful, just hard work, all business and mamma'll have dinner waiting when you're done.

"Jib first," I yelled to Danny and before I could move, he was gone forward to loose the jib sail. I started loosing the ties on the main, and when Danny came back, I swung the bow to starboard into the wind and we both hauled, he on the main and I on the jib. I didn't even have to tell him which line to use. He beat me, too. Had the main sail up and set before I finished hauling the jib. I swung back on course, loosed the main boom as she came around and watched her heel to port, cut the engine and went to work on the mizzen. We were sailing as we should be, no engine, just sail and I experienced a thrill, as I always do, when the sails draw full, the hull bites deep into the waves and she takes off like the thoroughbred she was built to be. A few minor adjustments and we settled in for a hard, cold trip. Danny took the wheel while Ginger and I put on foul weather gear down below. There was something really odd seeing that beautiful body swallowed up in the bulk of the storm suit. Then we put our sou'wester hats on and had a good laugh.

"When you said we'd have fun, O'Keefe, you weren't kidding. This goes beyond fun. Next time we go sailing I'll just bring an umbrella and skip all this fashionable storm suit stuff."

"You may be thankful for that suit before the night's over. I gave her a kiss and a pat on the rear." She looked troubled for a moment.

"Will there be another time, Bill? I mean, will you take me sailing again after all this?"

"You bet. Don't lose your confidence now. You're doing just fine."

The boat took an especially big wave and fell off to port, rolling violently and sending us flying against the port side bunk. Water poured through the main hatch. I scrambled up and rushed on deck to find Danny clinging to the stanchions. I gave him a hand up and back into the cockpit.

"Took a rogue wave. Didn't see it coming...sorry..." He was choking and spitting seawater.

"It's alright, Danny. I should have been on deck. I'll take the helm for a while. Go below and dry out." He shook his head but I insisted. It was time to get serious and not take any more chances. I tied a harness on Ginger and one for myself and snapped lifelines to the harness belts. If we went overboard, the lines would keep us with the boat. It was pitch black and growing colder The wind was getting up and we were heeled to port with the rails under water. Everything was working fine so far and even in this wind, which I estimated at twenty-five knots or better, the old girl was handling like a charm. The yawl design was doing its job with very little weather helm. Time passed and the seas were getting up a bit too much. I was about to reef when Danny appeared back on deck.

"Sorry about that, Mr. O'Keefe. Dad said not to be a burden."

"You're not, Danny. I've taken a few waves I never saw coming. Then again, I've been hit by a few waves I did see. There's no justice out here."

We pounded along on a close reach for two hours until light started to break behind us in the east. Visibility was less than a mile and the wind was whipping up, shifting to the north.

"Danny, how much longer do you think this wind will hold?"

"Till noon, then more west."

"We should be in by then if everything holds together."

"Yup." A man of few words.

Another hour and we had to reef down, no easy job in a forty-knot breeze. Danny confirmed my estimate. Seas were choppy, crossed with changing winds and tides so we were taking more water over the bow, but the storm suits did their job and we remained relatively comfortable.

"Gardiners." Danny pointed forward to a low-lying mass of land off the port bow, right on track. Jake's heading plus a few adjustments had brought us right at the northern point of the island. Our spirits picked up as we cleared the tip of Gardiners and then Ginger showed up on deck with a jug of milk and a box of Fig Newtons.

"Figured you guys must be starved. I sure am." She was back into her stewardess role. I waited another half hour and called in.

"Green Marine. This is the Gentle Spirit, over."

"Gentle Spirit, Green Marine, what's your position?" Tom was still on duty. The man never slept.

"We're by Garidners. Give us another hour and we'll be there. Any word about Harry?"

"Negative, is there anything we can do for you?"

"Yes, I'll want to leave right away when I arrive. Can you take care of the boat? Also, arrange for transport of one able bodied seaman back to Block Island."

"Can do. We've got some hot coffee and muffins waiting."

Time was running out for all of us. It had stopped for Harry Dondi and might never go again. There was really no need to rush back to East Harbour. I didn't want to go back into the Berman case unprepared. I needed backup and the sort of help I had in mind was not easy to find. Also, I needed a plan but most of all, I needed a shave, shower and something warm to eat. Beyond that, it was simple legwork and watching my backside.

We rounded the northern tip of Shelter Island and charged down the channel under full sail. I rounded up right at the main dock, all standing, and everyone scrambled to haul down the sails, set the bumpers and tie off to the dock. Tom Green and Timmy along with several other hands jumped to help us and in no time everything was secured. I was able to relax and take a breather for the first time in hours. The voyage was over and now the transition had to be made back to dry land. Just walking requires a different set of muscles and a special effort at coordination. I was sitting in the cockpit, coiling a line while Ginger gathered her gear below, when some character about 6'6", 280 pounds, black beard and hair, stepped on board without being invited. He stood before me and started yelling.

"YHO! Ginger! Where the hell are you? Ginger! " She stuck her head out the main hatch.

"Buddy? What are you doing here? You're supposed to be in Chicago."

"I called Marty last night and he said you weren't there. When he said you went sailing, I caught a flight to New York and rented a car. Now tell me what the hell's going on. What are you up to now?"

"Nothing, Buddy! We just went sailing, that's all. Mr. O'Keefe was very nice. He let me go along on his boat to learn how to sail. You should try it. It's fantastic!" She stepped through the hatch, short shorts too small, wearing one of my short-sleeved shirts with the monogram, WTO, on the pocket, top two buttons undone and no bra. She was barefooted, her face wind burned, a picture of pure loveliness. It didn't help my case at all.

"Nothing, huh? You sure don't look dressed for sailin', Bitch. You been messin' around on me?"

"No, Buddy! Now just settle down and come with me." She stepped past me, taking him by the arm in an attempt to get him off the boat but good ole' Buddy would have nothing to do with it.

He jerked away from Ginger's grasp and spun on me.

"You O'Keefe?"

I guess my face said it all. Now, I'm not a small man but he was big and strong. He grabbed the front of my slicker, lifted me right off my seat and punched me in the face. I saw it coming and managed to turn my head so his fist glanced off my cheekbone. That probably wouldn't have been the end of it but for Ginger, who stepped in: I should say, jumped in. She jumped right on Buddy's back and put a chokehold around his neck. It was a big neck but Ginger was a strong girl. I can attest to that, and she managed to divert his attention just enough to let me get loose and off the boat onto the dock where more trouble was waiting for me.

"Hello, Bill. How was your trip?" Connie Wilson stood facing me, feet spread, hands on her hips. My first thought was nice hips.

"Fraught with danger, I think." I felt my cheekbone. "There are many unknown dangers associated with the sport of sailing."

"I'll bet! And how was Ginger?" Connie had a smirk on her face but there was a flash of fire in her eyes.

"She had a confidence problem but I think she's finally solved it." Ginger had Buddy down on his knees in the cockpit of the yawl, her chokehold still firmly locked around his neck. Tom Green and his boys stood on the dock cheering her on. I gave her a silent cheer, myself.

"Yes, I'll bet she had a problem and you helped her, didn't you?"

"Honest, Connie. She did it all herself. Sailing does that for you."

"Really? You'll have to take me sometime… Sailing, that is. But only if you have the time!"

"Right, I'd like that. By the way, who is this fellow, Buddy?"

"Oh, she didn't tell you?" Buddy is Ginger's husband. He's a pilot for Trans Air and they see each other, sort of, like ships passing in the dark. Only, this time her ship sailed without him and he's very upset. I tried to warn you but he jumped on your boat and started yelling 'Ginger', 'Ginger'." She mimicked Buddy.

"Alright, Connie. I surrender. What do I have to do to make

peace?"

"You'll surrender when and if I say so. Until then, you will suffer and feel guilty."

"Yes, mamm." I turned to find Ginger leading Buddy off the boat toward us. I braced for another attack but it never came.

"Buddy wants to apologize to you, Bill...Apologize, Buddy!" She whacked him across the arm. He looked embarrassed.

"I'm sorry, Mr. O'Keefe. Ginger was just telling me everything you did for her. She said you was the perfect gentleman. I wanna thank you for helpin' her with that confidence thing. Man! She never stood up to me that way before. You're awright, man." He stuck out his paw and I shook it, watching my hand disappear into his big, clammy, hand. His face was red and he was shaking all over. Ginger has that effect on men. I can testify to that.

"Buddy and me are going to spend a couple of days together in New York City, sorta like a honeymoon. Thanks loads, O'Keefe. We'll have to do it again sometime." She winked and they walked off together. So help me, she actually winked right in front of everyone.

"Come on, O'Keefe," said Connie. "I can't say 'lets do it again sometime', so I have to just say come on." She took hold of the collar of my slicker and pulled me toward the parking lot. "So...come on." Like I said, when one has been at sea, the transition to land can be very tricky. ❊

CHAPTER ELEVEN

Tom Green gave us hot coffee and muffins. He and his crew were hosing down the decks of the Gentle Spirit and covering the sails as I drove away with Connie following in her car. I drove slowly, giving my reflexes time to catch up. My equilibrium was still stuck several hours back in the darkness, miles from nowhere, surrounded by crashing waves and howling winds. Every time I turned the wheel, I instinctively leaned opposite the direction of the turn to correct for heel. I still wore my foul weather suit and the .44 Magnum in a shoulder holster, so I wasn't comfortable. I knew this would pass. The plan was to stop at my cottage, pick up my "tools", leave the Caddy and continue in Connie's car. I didn't want Myron Gates to know I was in town until the time was right and the advantage mine. The rain was letting up but roads were still awash with running water and large puddles.

We turned off the main road onto a narrow lane running across a potato field, through a stand of tall white pines to the sand dunes. There were open gates in the fence at the end of the road, marking the beginning of the wildlife refuge. From the small turn around at the end of the blacktop to the cottage was about 300 yards across sandy dunes with occasional scrub oak and pine trees dotting the landscape. There were no walkways. But the area wasn't totally closed to the public. Signs warned trespassers not to drive vehicles past the fence; no digging for shellfish, spear fishing, fishing with nets and no lights. No picnics, fires, camping, drinking of alcoholic beverages or flying of kites. The result was very little traffic.

So, when I stopped the Caddy and saw the tire tracks across the sand, I knew we had visitors. Maybe some teenagers were looking for a place to neck. Do they still do that? Poachers might be looking for clams or bird eggs but most locals knew better. The place was too closely watched. Perhaps, it was duck hunters from the city who didn't care where they went? It didn't really matter. I had to treat the presence of an intruder with caution. Even with the wind and rain, the tracks were still visible, going one way, no return, so they might still be there. I had the .44 Magnum and a full box of cartridges in my tote bag. It's an awesome weapon and not really practical for everyday use because of its kick. It requires a strong arm and a steady nerve to withstand the recoil of a handheld weapon of such power. I had both and a lot of experience using it. There were bigger guns but this would do.

"We have company so stay behind me and do as I say." I pointed to the tire tracks in the sand. It was better to keep Connie with me.

"Do you really need that gun, Bill? They're probably just kids looking for a place to neck. Do they still do that sort of thing?"

"I was going to ask you. When kids go to a secluded spot now, it's to transact a major drug deal or to hide the body that was the result of the last one."

"You're too cynical, O'Keefe."

"Maybe I've just seen too much. Anyway, let's be careful. We're visible from the cottage so if someone is there, they've probably seen us."

We started walking, sinking over the tops of our shoes in the loose, wet sand. I led the way, crouching down, weaving around the small hillocks of sand, offering as small a target as possible. We came within a hundred yards of the back of the cottage before I saw a movement at one of the three back windows in the guest room. They broke out a pane of glass and started shooting before I could say "duck". I hit the dirt, but Connie stood there in total disbelief so I grabbed her legs and pulled, dumping her on her backside in the sand.

"Ouch! You brute. I would have gotten down without your help."

"Someday, you'll thank me." I pulled the .44 Magnum from under my slicker.

"This is ridiculous, you know. We shouldn't have to worry about being shot at like this. This is a free country and there are laws against people carrying guns around like that."

She sat there very proud of herself, having delivered her speech in a timely fashion, effectively pointing the finger at me like it was all my fault, and if I wasn't carrying a gun, then nobody else would be carrying a gun and the world would be a safe place and so on. Meanwhile, the battle raged on. They had some heavy guns and a couple of them were automatic assault rifles. I recognized the sharp, staccato beat of the M16.

"Look, Sweetheart! I didn't start this war, but I'm damn sure going to finish it, so if you're through with your speech on gun control, law and order, and other current events, what say we find a better place to hide? Those bullets are coming a bit too close for comfort."

I motioned for her to follow and crawled off to the left toward a higher pile of sand with some grass on the top. But the wind was blowing straight into my face, so when I looked over the sand dune I got a face full of rain, wind, sand, and salt spray, enough to blind me. Poor planning. They had pistols, the two assault rifles and a small caliber rifle, maybe a .22 caliber like the one in my gun chest but the bullets were real.

"Why don't you shoot them back, Bill? Use your gun, for crying out loud." Spoken like a true gun lover.

"Connie, that's my home. Every bullet hole I put in it will have to be filled and repainted. Frankly, I'm tired of painting and wall-papering."

"Oh, hell, O'Keefe! I'll help you paint the whole damn place. Just shoot the bastards. We can't stay out here all day. Look at me. I'm getting wet and I have sand all over me. I need a shower. Do you always treat a girl this way the first time she comes to your house?"

She was slipping into shock but she had a point.

I waited for a lull in the firing and stood, leveled my weapon and squeezed off a round. It hit about six inches to the right of where I was aiming. Not bad for a one hundred yard shot. I cocked and leveled again, squeezed off another shot but didn't see it hit.

"Geeze, O'Keefe! That thing is a cannon. Are you sure it's legal?"

"Probably not, but then none of this is legal." I rolled over to the end of the dune and came up in a kneeling position, cocked the gun and leveled it but didn't fire. I heard an engine start, doors slam and the crunching of gears. I stood up, shucked the two empty shells and reloaded. The engine was winding out and I caught a glimpse of the top of a vehicle, then it popped up and over a small dune, coming right at me. It was a green Jeep with a big aerial whipping around on the back. The sides were open and someone behind the driver was leaning out with an assault rifle. He started firing in short bursts, like they teach you in basic training. My sergeant in Vietnam said that was a pile of bull. "If you're in a firefight and you can see the enemy coming at you, and you got any brains left, you don't fire in short bursts. You pull the friggin trigger and kill the bastards till they're all dead or you're all dead. Do you understand?" He was right.

I raised my good arm, aiming at the front of the Jeep, leveled, cocked and fired...leveled, cocked and fired...leveled, cocked and fired. One of my shots hit the engine and it literally exploded, sending pieces of the castings flying everywhere. The hood flew open, the windshield blew out and the driver lost control. The Jeep swerved right, climbed up and over a small dune, went airborne, nose dived into the next sand dune, flipped over and exploded just like in the movies. I always thought that business of the car catching on fire when it goes off the road in the movies was baloney, but there it was. The Jeep was flipped upside down on fire with no survivors. I found Connie behind me, transfixed by the sight of the burning vehicle. The look of horror on her face shook me more than the burning Jeep.

"Are...are...they...dead?" I put my good arm on her shoulder and turned her around.

"We're alive, Babe. That's all that matters."

I walked her to the cottage porch and put her in the wicker rocker next to the front door. It was the same chair where Willie Monk sat. I reloaded the .44 Magnum and stepped carefully through the front door. The place was a mess. They went through everything, but my special hiding place was undisturbed. I checked the rest of house. The body was in the guest room at the back of the cottage. He must have been standing directly in front of the windows. Only two panes of glass were missing and the bullet hit him dead center in the chest. My .22 caliber Remington pump was in his hands, resting in his lap and he was sitting on the floor, back against the wall, staring wide eyed into the distance as though he didn't believe what happened. The reason I knew he was standing in front of the window was because that's where his shoes were. Black oxford, highly polished loafers. He sat there with nothing on his feet but white cotton socks.

"Is he dead?" Connie stood in the doorway.

"You should go back outside and watch the rain fall, Connie. This will give you nightmares."

"Does it give you...nightmares?" She started to cry.

"Sometimes but after awhile it goes away." He had no wallet, just a leather pouch with a badge and a picture I.D. identifying him as Sergeant Oscar Cirrelli, Reserve Police, Town of East Harbour.

"He's one of Myron's reserve cops." I handed the I.D. to Connie. "Oh no, Bill! This will cause a lot of trouble."

"In more ways than you can imagine, my fine lady. This is just what I need to bring the heat down on Myron Gates." There was an explosion outside, like a big whoosh.

"The gas tank on the Jeep just exploded. They'll have a time of it identifying the bodies." I pushed Connie out into the living room and I closed the door to the guest room. "Come on, let's get out of here."

"Let me help you clean up this mess."

"We'll have to leave it for the authorities. My cell phone is dead. I have a car phone. You'd better come with me."

"I wouldn't stay here alone for anything. Not with ...that...thing in there." Her entire body shuddered.

We walked back out to the car, avoiding the burning Jeep by a couple of dunes. I started the car to boost the transmitter, opened my address book to the correct page and dialed the number. It was a secure line with limited access. I was one of the privileged.

"State Police. Lieutenant Hank Gaines." He sounded the same as always. I'd known him since Vietnam.

"Hank, this is Bill O'Keefe." I put it on speaker.

"Well! Speak of the devil. We've just been talking about you, old son. I think we need to get together."

"More than you can imagine, Hank. Bring your mops and buckets. I got four of them for you."

"What the hell's goin' on, O'Keefe? First, I get a call from this fella, Myron Gates...let's see, says he's Chief of Police, some place called East Harbour. Says you're the prime suspect in a one-man crime wave. Says you attacked and robbed three of his best men working undercover. Says you shot an insurance salesman and dumped him alongside the highway. So, what's happening out there? Who do I believe?"

"Believe what you see. His three goons jumped me in the parking lot of the Daylight Inn. Came at me across twenty yards of lighted parking lot, ragged formation. Not smart. There was a fourth. It was Chief Myron Gates. He fired some shots and ran away."

"Sounds like the time we were in Hi Phong Harbor. Same results too. We really showed 'em that time."

"Hi Phong was a long time ago. I got sliced pretty bad this time."

"Getting old, son?"

"He was too fast. My mistake."

"I hear he's not movin' so fast anymore and this Chief of Police, what's his name...Myron...he wants your scalp."

"Listen, I think this thing today might have been a hit ordered by Myron Gates. The arrest warrant is just a smoke screen. You could do me a real big favor if you kept it quiet like until I have a chance to do some hound-doggin around. I'm at my place and it's a mess."

"No shit? Are you talkin' dirty cops? Okay then, I can take jurisdiction because I been called by Mr. Gates but I need more to keep control, so stay there and I'll be to your place...let's say in about forty five-minutes. We'll keep it off the air."

"Great, and thanks."

A trooper pulled up behind the Caddy about fifteen minutes later. He got out of the car with a riot gun and walked slowly up to the driver's window. I put my hands on top of the steering wheel and stopped breathing.

"Move real slow, mister. Out of the car. Keep your hands where I can see them."

"Take it easy, Officer. Everything's cool." He was young. I did as he said. Connie stayed put.

"Your name William O'Keefe?" He pointed the riot gun at my belly and started patting me down.

"There's a Sturm-Ruger .44 Magnum under my coat, Son, so don't get excited." I opened my coat and let him take the gun.

"Man, what a cannon. You got a permit?" He backed up but kept the riot gun pointed at my belly button. I decided not to move.

"Yes, I have a permit for it and I'm friendly so how about you put that shotgun away and take it easy. Nothing's going to happen. Okay?" He hesitated, then slowly lowered the shotgun.

"They said there was a shooting here and I was to secure the area. They didn't say what to do with you."

"So, don't do anything. My name is Bill O'Keefe. What's your name?"

"Philip Rhodes...ahh, Trooper Rhodes."

"Look, Phil, can I call you Phil?" He nodded. "Do you know Lt. Hank Gaines?" He nodded again. "Well, Hank and me go way back and he's on his way here to take charge. I called him so I know he'll be here, he said in forty-five minutes, and when he arrives, he'll explain everything." He nodded again. "So, ahh, Phil, would it be all right if I got back into my car and waited there instead of out here in the rain? I just don't want to get any wetter than I am, Okay?" He nodded and looked at the .44 Magnum in his hand.

"I'll keep this until Lt. Gaines arrives, Sir."

"Fine, that's just fine. Hey, that's a real good idea." He nodded again and walked to his car. I got back into the Caddy with Connie.

"What was that all about?"

"Training exercise. These fellows deal mostly with traffic control. They're not used to dealing with murder and mayhem like the rest of us." I dialed the phone again. This time I knew the number by heart. It rang seven times.

"State Mutual," a sexy voice came back at me.

"John Stanley, please. This is O'Keefe. Patch me through." I was calling the New York office. I waited for maybe three minutes.

"Bill! Bill O'Keefe. My boy, how are you?"

"I'm just great, John, and you?"

"Oh, not bad. Actually, I could use some good news for a change. Things seem to be out of control in East Harbour. You are in East Harbour, aren't you? Too bad about Harry. He should have let you handle things, but I'm glad you called, Bill. So you've decided to accept my offer. Let's face it, twenty-five G's for a couple days work is pretty good pay. Harry couldn't wait to jump at the chance to make that kind of money. Well, everything is all right now and you'll give me a report by tomorrow morning, right? Look, Bill, nice of you to call but I'm in the middle of a meeting with the Board right now and we have a full agenda. I'll just hand you back to my secretary and you can give her whatever you need to, all right?"

"No!"

"What? Bill, we really need to work as a team here. You know the score, so..."

"Shut up, John!" I spoke in an even voice.

"Bill..."

"Shut up and listen, damn you! I know you have it on speaker and you're trying to make things look good but they aren't and there are some things I need you to do. Only you can do this, John. Do you hear me?"

"I hear you, Bill. But what's the problem?"

"John, I work for 10% because I'm good and you need me. I don't work for $25,000 because that doesn't even cover expenses. I put three men in the hospital the other night and got myself cut up in the process. Those three men were local reserve police in East Harbour. I just killed four more like them. Harry Dondi was probably shot and left for dead by some of the same bunch of local cops. We're dealing with a real bad situation here, John, and I need you to do something for me, NOW! Do you hear me?"

"Yes...ahh...Okay. What is it, Bill? I've got the Board here, and..."

"Oh, shut up and listen. You remember three years ago when you played golf with the Governor of the State, Paola Cantelli?"

Paul...you mean, Paul Cantelli?"

"Yes, John. He changed it to Paul for obvious reasons. Have you kept in touch with him?"

"Yes, of course. I keep in touch with all those guys. Never know when we might need one of 'em for a little favor." I could hear laughter in the background.

"John! I want you to call Governor Cantelli and collect a little favor. I want you to call him right now and tell him what's going on in East Harbour. Act outraged. You can do it. Tell the Governor that East Harbour is rotten, that two of your investigators have been attacked by local police in East Harbour and that you need protection. Ask him to take jurisdiction and send in an investigative team. Tell him Lt. Hank Gaines is already investigating an attempted hit on one of your investigators today, right now, even as we speak. Okay, John?"

"Are you serious? He'll think I'm crazy. I can't do that. What if it backfires and what you said isn't true or something? How do you think that will look?"

"How do you think it's going to look to the whole world if an investigator from State Mutual gets himself shot and thrown into a roadside ditch while checking out a six million dollar life insurance scam in a small Long Island bedroom community? Do you want people to think they can just shoot your people on sight? Hell, John, the streets won't be safe for life insurance salesmen. We can't allow terrorist attacks on our insurance industry." There was silence on the line.

"Does this mean you'll take over the case if I talk to the Governor, Bill?"

"Yes, usual terms, 10% and I'll bail you out." Silence again.

"Ahh...sorry, Bill. I'll talk to the Governor but the Board won't go along with the 10%. New policy. We can't afford to be intimidated by freelancers like you. Nothing personal. It's a policy shift. Sorry!"

"Does this mean you'll issue the six million dollar claim check to the grieving widow, John?"

"Yes, I guess it does. We like to stand behind our people, even in a case like this where it will cost us money." My heart jumped a beat.

"Gee whiz, John. Harry Dondi will be pleased to hear you say that." I disconnected and sat there, trying to control my excitement.

"I can't believe that man. Bill, is he serious when he says they'll issue a six million dollar check rather than pay you 10% to stop the claim?"

"Something is very rotten in State Mutual. He fell for it, Connie. John Stanley is motivated by saving face and now there's $6 million in the pot instead of just 10%." ❋

CHAPTER TWELVE

The $25,000 was meant for me. Harry Dondi was in East Harbour because he was afraid of losing his job. They could stop the payment of the $6 million just on the discrepancies in the application and medical report, and if the beneficiary wanted to sue, then let her. State Mutual was not afraid of a lawsuit. So nothing made sense. The thought occurred to me that I'd made a mistake by calling John Stanley. Sure, I found out about the payoff but now he knew I was back on the case.

I told Connie about John as we sat watching the rain and wind driving the gulls around the sky. He was my supervisor when I worked as a life insurance salesman in White Plains before Vietnam. We went door-to-door selling worthless whole-life insurance policies. We concentrated on the older people and the poor blacks down in the center of town, climbing three and four story flights of stairs to knock on doors with no locks, the smell of leaking gas, grease and garbage overpowering our senses, making it hard to breath. We went for the collectables, the weekly and monthly finance policies where the agent kept going back to collect nickels and dimes every month off widows and old people who couldn't read or write. The face amount of the policies never amounted to much, maybe $300-$500 with an occasional $1,000. John showed me how to judge the amount by the surroundings and the amount of cash the client could show us.

"Don't oversell 'em, Billy. They'll drop the policy if you gouge 'em too bad in the beginning. We wanna bleed 'em a little bit at a time and then resell 'em later when the time is ripe."

And we did. We sold mother's policies to sons and son's policies to mothers and widow's coverage to daughters and then John showed me one I'd never seen. This old black lady had a policy on her husband and he died. So, John filed the claim, drew a check for $250 payable to the widow. He took the check, had the widow endorse it and sold her another policy for $1000 with a different company. In those days, a salesman could represent several companies. Then he back dated the new policy two months and filed it. In about three weeks it came back and he waited another two months, took the death certificate, changed the date and filed the claim for $1000, drew the check, went to the widow and had her sign it, promising to bring the money right back. Now he had $1250, and he kept the whole amount plus the commissions. After a year or so he went back to the old lady, who didn't recognize him, and started all over again. That was my first lesson involving insurance fraud.

I went to work for State Mutual again after Vietnam and we picked up right where we left off. He still thought he was the teacher but I was a different pupil. John became manager of the New York City office and then he convinced enough people to back him for a junior V.P. job in Omaha. He was considered a brilliant up-and-coming financial wizard when he went to Omaha. Actually, he just had a few friends in the brokerage houses that were privy to insider trading information and he took advantage of those connections to make some money for the company and himself. I was never certain how much he made for himself and how much went to the company or even how much of what he made was the company's money.

I rode his coattails on a few tips and made a bundle. That was before computers became sophisticated and the social security number was tacked onto everyone's file. If a person even sneezes now, it's recorded and the tax sharks are on your back. So John Stanley made his bundle and he moved up the ladder to the Board where guys like him didn't care any more about anyone. That was a mistake, because John and the Board had never met Willie Monk.

I was the assistant manager of the New York Claims Division, when I became aware of a short, dark haired, dark-complexioned, Armenian fellow who would occasionally show up in our department, take over someone's desk or office, and start working on stacks of papers. He never said "hello", "excuse me", "may I please", or "goodbye". Just "where's dis", or "what's dat?" Finally, my curiosity got hold of my mouth and I asked one of the old timers about him.

"Oh, him. That's Willie Monk, company investigator. He don't bother nobody and nobody wants nothing to do with him," and she walked off.

During the next few days, I watched him move in and out of my domain until a Friday night when I was alone, working late, and in walks Willie Monk, sits down in the chair next to my desk, lights up a stogie and blows smoke in my face.

"You been watchin' me, young fella!"

"You're in my department." I blew the smoke away.

"My job!" He blew some more in my face.

"My job is to know what goes on around me."

"Either you're curious about what I'm doin or you're dirty. Most of the ones dat's dirty, avoid me or they look real guilty and turn away. You don't look guilty and you don't turn away."

"And I don't smoke either, so blow it the other way or I'll toss your ass out the window."

"Sorry, just a technique I use to get people off balance." He blew the other way. "These things are the worst smokes in the world, but they shorten conversations. Nobody likes talkin with a stogie in his face, even if he smokes."

"You're right, Mr. Monk. No one in his right mind would want you around for very long with that thing. So, what the hell do you want?"

"Well, I'm gonna take a chance on you, Mr. O'Keefe, and I'm gonna trust you. Can I trust you?" I said nothing. "You see, I think you're an honest man, more or less, and there's a problem right here in this department that needs fixin' right away. I'm hopeful you can help me."

"What is it, Mr. Monk? I'm a busy man!"

"Yeh, well, you're gonna be a lot busier if you don't watch it, cause somebody's gonna nail yah for fraud and charge yah with grand theft, to the tune of maybe $15 million or better."

"And I suppose that somebody is you, right? My grandmother always said if you weren't guilty, you have nothing to worry about."

"Listen to me. Your grandmother never worked in dis zoo. I don't think you're guilty but you're gonna get nailed cause your name's on the claim approvals." My mouth was suddenly very dry.

"My name's on everything. It's like a blanket approval. Each individual processor checks the claim, approves or disapproves and passes it to an adjuster. If the adjuster disagrees, he or she writes a letter. If not, they sign my name, a check is issued and the claim is filed."

"And who checks the adjusters?"

"I do. We have a compliance team that goes through everything and matches up the results with the paperwork in the files."

"How often?"

"Every six months...or a year...I think."

"Right! When's the last time you did dis? A year ago? Two years?"

"I don't know. I'm quoting from my Procedures Manual. I never actually did it in the year and a half I've been here. They keep me so busy with grunt work I don't even have time for my family."

"May I show you something, Mr. O'Keefe? Let me use your computer terminal for a moment. Also, please open your New York City phone directory to the 'H' section." He punched a format for the weekly claims paid list and waited for the computer to access the list.

"Now, if you'll notice, the list of claims paid out has an unusually large number of names starting with the letter 'H'. Cross-reference, if you will, the names in the telephone directory on pg. 235, right there...see dat? The last names in the directory are the same as on the claims list except that the first names are different. Now, go down ten names and do a match up. See? The tenth first name is now matched up with the first last name and so it goes right on down through the H's for over fifty claims. There's eight legitimate claims in the H's. All the rest is bogus and you approved every one of dem yourself, Mr. O'Keefe." I said nothing. I just sat there and gawked like a country bumpkin at a county fair.

"I can see you're surprised. Well, dat's good. Dat's very good, Mr. O'Keefe. If you weren't surprised, I'd be very disappointed in my judgment of you. Wait until you see this." He typed some more keys and the screen displayed the 'H' list with addresses. "Dis is where it really gets obvious. See, all the 'H' claims except the eight I pointed out, have the same P.O. box number. Now, I ask you, how could fifty people all just happen to live in the same post office box? What a coincidence."

"But...but, that's...that's stupid. Anyone would know he'd be caught doing such a dumb trick. The compliance team would catch that one right away."

"Give it some thought. Who decides what the compliance team examines. Better yet, who decides when to do a Compliance Audit?"

"My boss, Manager of Claims, Jeff Gold." I felt numb all the way to my toes. "How could he do it? There's over a half million in this month alone. He must be stealing millions."

"Your average payout per month," continued Willie, as if teaching a second grade class, "is over $18 million just in this department alone. Jeff Gold has kept his theft under 2½ % for the last three years. He's got about $15 million stashed in various New York City banks. He's started to transfer some of it to Swiss accounts and that's the part that worries me. We may never see dat money again."

"Well, we've got to stop this. Have him arrested and make him give it all back."

"That aint how it works. The company don't want a scandal. People don't like insurance companies that mismanage their money. So, here's what we're gonna do."

Willie had waited until Friday night to make his move. He was a genius with a computer and what he showed me that night opened up a whole new world. He'd broken the codes of every bank in Manhattan where Jeff Gold had placed money. He showed me the readouts he had and now, tonight, he would transfer those monies out of Gold's accounts into special reserve accounts that belonged to State Mutual. A lot of transfers like this were made on Friday nights and banks often removed their security measures to speed up the processing of their business. Otherwise, they would never get their work done. Friday night was a good time to pull off an illegal transfer.

"You see dis account right here? The V.P. of Finance in dis bank was supposed to delete his code after making that entry right there but he forgot or got interrupted or something. That code is still good and I'm gonna use it to clean out Jeff Gold's accounts and return the money to us where it belongs. Come Monday morning, I'll have Gold's ass on the carpet in the General Manager's office and I'll make the son of a bitch pray for a quick death."

We worked together that night for the first time. Monday morning in the General Manager's office I watched Willie intimidate Jeff Gold into revealing his Swiss bank account numbers. Then we transferred the monies back to our company accounts. I was promoted to Claims Manager and given $100 a week raise. That's when it finally dawned on me that I was in the wrong job. Willie was really the one who convinced me. We worked together for the next three years, digging out the scum and rot of fraud wherever it existed inside the company. I got high on it.

Then, one day, Willie came to me with a problem. Investments were being made and contracts were being let out by the commercial department of the company, involving millions. Nothing new, it was listed in the company's annual report. But what had Willie going was the loss factor. He did a computer analysis of the investment and loss ratio of the company's projects and compared them to those of a similar nature in other companies in the industry. State Mutual was maybe a tenth to a quarter of a percent off. I thought he was losing it but he kept on until I started to believe him. He cracked the computer codes in several banks and insurance companies, not to mention three of the biggest secondary mortgage holding companies in the country and he traced a similar pattern through all of them. Initially, he thought it was just a standard practice, but then he realized it was one person dealing with all the companies he had investigated. Mr. 'X' was the name we gave him.

"Look at dis, Billy. Every one of these projects has payments to the SARTXE Corp. but there is no such company. It just don't exist, but if you look at it backwards, SARTXE spells EXTRAS. Get it? All these payments are EXTRAS. Someone has a crazy sense of humor. Thing is, every time I go to look dis company up, it disappears."

So, we started checking SARTXE Corp in the company records and elsewhere for the next year. We chased all over the place, tripping over leads and clues, hunting them down, losing them and picking them up again. We could be seen in the public library, the city clerk's office, the Office of Corporate Records in Albany, half the banks in Manhattan, the Insurance Commissioner's office, you name it. We tracked Mr. 'X' all over the place and Willie was right. We'd find a clue, let's say a $100,000 consulting fee, paid by check #10328, from Concrete Posts Inc. to SARTXE Inc. and it shows up on the company's records Monday afternoon. Tuesday morning, the payment was gone off the records and the amount would be transferred to another account, buried in general expenses. Payments were always electronically transferred with a window implanted to wipe it out within twenty-four hours.

We traced some payments to the Credit Reporting Consultants, Inc. in Chicago, an industry credit reporting company, buried about three levels below the surface of the secondary mortgage holding market, a gray area of finance. The trail disappeared there with no record whatsoever. Willie suspected the payments were connected to the financing arrangements of each project, but we never found out because of an unexpected change in events.

"So what happened?" Connie was staring at me, intently.

"I don't think anyone knew for sure that it was Willie or me tracking Mr. 'X' but somebody got nervous. Let's face it, whoever was doing this was a real computer whiz, smarter than either of us, so when we accessed someone else's computer, we ran the risk of getting caught."

The rain outside the car was letting up but the wind was still pretty stiff, and I was wondering if Connie really cared about all this.

"John Stanley became president of State Mutual and the board voted to hire and employ only college graduates. Willie Monk was given early retirement and I quit out of protest. Willie always thought John Stanley was Mr. 'X' but I told him John wasn't smart enough. Now, I don't know. That was five years ago." Another trooper arrived.

"In just a few minutes, Connie, all hell is going to break loose. There will be cops stomping on top of cops all over the place and they'll all have one thing in common. They'll treat you like you're stupid and they're smart. They will ask you if I could have avoided killing those men. You answer anyway you chose, pretty lady."

"I think I can handle myself, Bill. The part I have trouble with is seeing those men burn. What a horrible way to die, but I guess you didn't plan that."

More cars were arriving. An ambulance arrived, lights flashing and in the midst of it all, the familiar figure of Hank Gaines was casually strolling down the middle of the road leading a forensics team with their black bags, followed by the photographer with his cameras, the EMT's with their stretchers, the county coroner with his stethoscope and a priest. I've always wondered why the coroner needed a stethoscope when his customers were already dead? Hank stopped to talk to trooper Rhodes who pulled out my .44 Magnum and handed it to him. He took the gun and turned toward us. Now the dance would begin.

"Hello, Bill. How's it hangin'?" We shook hands. Normally, we would have greeted each other with a high five but the situation seemed to require some decorum.

"Still doing what I do best, Hank, and you?"

"Me? I'm still climbing the ladder of success. Show me what's going on here." I did, all the way from the tire tracks to the dead cop in my guest room, to the burning Jeep. I explained the case to him and about Harry Dondi being shot and left for dead. I mentioned my telephone call to John Stanley. Hank spread his team out to cover the area.

"It looks like a battlefield here, O'Keefe. How the hell did you do so much damage with just five shots?"

"They did most of it themselves. The one in the house was pure luck. I didn't want to blow holes in my house. I just wanted them to get out of there and into the open. Instead of taking off down the beach, they came straight at me, guns blazing. That assault rifle is a vicious weapon, Hank. All they had to do was stop right next to the sand dune we were behind and blow us away."

"So you went head to head and blew them away instead, right?"

"I was lucky and you know it. One of my shots must have hit the engine and it exploded. The whole front end of the Jeep just disintegrated like it was made of plastic. The driver lost it and the thing blew up. I really didn't want them dead and burned. I needed a witness so we could find out what's going on. Right now, we have a case of possible insurance fraud and murder but every time I try to move, I run into this Myron Gates and his part time police goons. This group was obviously sent to kill me. If all they wanted was to search the house, they could have gotten a warrant. They could have escaped down the beach and I never would have known who they were."

"So, you're saying this was a hit and he was trying to wipe out witnesses in this Berman case?" I nodded agreement.

"Myron Gates insisted you were a dangerous criminal and should be shot on sight. That's why Trooper Rhodes acted the way he did. I smelled a rat right away but we have an administrative problem. The Governor received a phone call from the president of State Mutual Insurance, asking us to assume jurisdiction in this case. So, the Governor directed me to do so. Problem is, your friend John Stanley, who isn't really your friend, said you might be dangerous and somewhat of an embarrassment to State Mutual. He said we might want to hold you for awhile, like until the end of the week when this thing is all over. Then the Governor, his honorable Paola Cantelli, found out that you were responsible for seven casualties, count 'em my friend, S-E-V-E-N, four of which are dead, and he directed me to take you into custody pending further investigation. I'm sorry, Bill, you're gonna hafta come with us and cool it for awhile."

"Damn it, Hank! I don't need to spend the next three days cooling my heels while these people filch $6 million from an insurance company. You're playing right into their hands. I thought you would go into East Harbour to put a stop to this."

"And you get rich while I'm chasing crazies around, right? No thanks, O'Keefe. I can't cover your backside on this one. It'll be my neck if I let you loose. The body count is already too high."

"Body count? Body count? Man you ain't seen nothin yet. Wait until those people in East Harbour get their hands on the money. They'll start knocking people off all over the place and you know why? I'll tell you why, because too many people are in on this thing. It's like a community project. It's a conspiracy to defraud an insurance company and restore a group of conservative local rednecks to political and economic power in East Harbour. It's not a big dot on the map yet but it will be when half the population starts dying and nobody knows why."

"He's right." Connie chimed in. "Those people are very desperate and they'll do whatever they have to in order to protect their plan."

"Hank, what do buddies do for buddies?"

"That's not fair. This isn't Nam and we're not in uniform."

"Wrong, Hank! You said it yourself. This looks like a battlefield, well, it is, damn it! Only we know what we're fighting for here. In Nam, we didn't. The stakes here are very high. We're fighting for money. Myron Gates and his goons can't afford to leave any witnesses, so unless you're prepared to take responsibility for the safety of Connie and me as well as a lot of innocent people, you'd better get ready for a blood bath. I'm asking you, man to man, Hank. Buddies don't let buddies go uncovered." Hank Gaines looked at me, then Connie, then at the ocean.

"I gotta go up to the car and make a call. Miss, ahh, Connie, you're free to go. O'Keefe? I don't wanna see you leave any trail behind you, understand?" I nodded. He turned and walked away. I grabbed Connie's arm and pulled her inside the cottage.

"Here are my keys. Pick up the gear in my trunk, including the guns and ID's. Drive your car out to the highway, turn right, go about a half-mile to the stone bridge and wait. I'll meet you there."

"But, Bill, you'll be a fugitive."

"Not really. Hank will cover for me. Are you with me, pretty lady?"

"Yes, Okay." I kissed her and watched as she drove away."

Connie was quite a woman and I didn't like dragging her into this mess, but I had no choice. I went into the cottage and grabbed some clothes, stuffed them into a canvas boat bag, went to the bathroom, added my toothbrush and shaver plus a couple of towels. The forensic team was gone and the EMT's had removed the body from the guest room. I removed the bricks covering the safe, fed in the combination and opened the door. I retrieved the computer runs left by Dr. John Smith, my 9mm. Berreta with extra clips, a money belt containing cash, and my equipment vest, a sort of tool chest made out of fabric. I was soaking wet so I changed into dry clothes, grabbed a hat and windbreaker, stepped to the door and came face to face with trooper Rhodes, a gun in his hand.

"Mr. O'Keefe?" He raised the gun.

"Yes?" I raised my hands.

"This is your gun. Lt. Gaines told me to come down here and get your signature on a receipt saying this is your gun, and that we're taking it for evidence. He says you would understand the procedure, and I was lucky to be alive, and to apologize. I'm sorry. I didn't have any instructions at the time and I just did what I thought was right. I guess you two were together in Vietnam." He handed me a book of padded receipts. The top one was all filled out and ready for my signature. I signed it and handed it back to him.

"Yes, well, thank you."

"He said to stay with you and bring you back up to the cars when you're ready."

"Look...ahh, Phil. I've gotta change so I'll be right out, alright?" He nodded and stepped back as I closed the door.

Granddad put an escape hatch in the bedroom closet as a way out in case of fire. He used it to avoid detection when he didn't want to face grandmother. I opened it, looked around and saw no one, dropped the bag and let myself down. I was under the back corner of the house in a crawl space boxed in by wooden latticework. I crawled under the latticework, worked across the dunes and down to the beach. I caught an occasional glimpse of trooper Rhodes standing patiently on the front porch. Once I hit the beach and I was out of sight, I broke into a steady trot, not an easy feat with the deep sand, but I kept going as long as I could until my legs felt like rubber, then I slowed to a walk. Hank was a joker. He sent trooper Rhodes with the gun to cover his tail. Philip was about to learn a lesson in police work. Don't let your principle witness escape from right under your nose. At a half-mile I cut back up through the dunes and scrub pines to the highway. No sign of Connie. I waited maybe fifteen minutes before she came along. I flagged her down and off we went.

"What happened?" She looked terrified.

"I forgot which way to turn. I went left and after a few miles I decided maybe I should turn around, but there was a state trooper following me, so I kept going until I came to a gas station so I pulled in and got gas. The trooper kept going, so I came back, and there you were. Oh Bill, I'm not good at this cloak and dagger stuff. I'm sorry."

"Not to worry, Babe. You're doing just fine." I laid back and closed my eyes. The dance had just begun. ❈

CHAPTER THIRTEEN

We drove in silence with the rain pouring down in torrents and the road awash. Connie drove slower as we approached East Harbour. I was almost asleep when she pulled over to the side of the road onto the grass. I opened my eyes and looked at her.

"Bill! Something is very wrong."

"What's going on?" I couldn't afford to lose another hour, let alone a day. Time was essential. Connie was staring straight ahead as if mesmerized by the flap-clop, flap-clop of the windshield wipers.

"William Thackery O'Keefe! Why did you come into my life in a way and at a time when I wasn't ready for you? I had everything a woman of my age and talents could ever want. I thought I was better than all those bimbos who just chase around after any good-looking piece of meat that happens to walk by. I was married in Iowa to a childhood boyfriend, someone I grew up with. After three years, I realized I couldn't go on so I left him, his farm with its pigs, corn and cows. I broke his heart. I left Iowa and went to college, majored in business and landed a job with Daylight Inns as a market analyst. I put all my energies into my career and that solved my social problems. Now, you're here and I'm feeling things I've never felt before." She turned and put her hand on mine. "I need to know if I'm here because you need someone to help or because you feel something special for me like I do for you and you're with me because you want to be...Oh Damn...I'm not doing this very well! I just want to know if I'll ever see you again after this is over?"

I leaned over and gave her a good strong kiss on the lips. "I won't lie to you, Connie. I need your help. If you weren't here, I'd do it alone, but differently. At another time and place I'd call you up and make a date, knock at your door with roses and show you my mother's picture. I'd take you to dinner, ply you with wine, dance the night away, take you home, and put you to bed. Then I would cook your breakfast and probably propose. As it is, there's a chance we may not make it to our next breakfast and I feel guilty about getting you involved in this mess...and yes, I want to see a lot of you after this is over, if you still want to."

"Will you take me sailing?"

"Yes...that too." She hesitated for a moment.

"Was she good, Bill? You don't have to answer that. I guess I just want to know how you look at women, what they mean to you. Like, a girl from Iowa could get an inferiority complex next to that Ginger."

"Yes, she was good and no it was not fun, especially when big old Buddy started beating on me. I guess I built myself a lifestyle after the divorce where I was isolated from getting hurt. The only real friend I had was Willie Monk, and when he got sick, I pulled back from people in general. That's how I solved the problem of my social life. When you first met me, you saw a man whose life was very neatly controlled and well defined. That's no longer the case because I have to consider how we will fit together in the future. I like the idea and I hope it works. Yes, Ginger was good and no it was not fun because it was meaningless. She lied and that hurt."

"I know what you mean and thanks for your honesty. I like that."

She kissed me back, leaned against her seat and said. "Now, where do we go and what do we do first?"

She had asked a good question. I went charging into East Harbour before, thinking they were small time hicks and the old pro, that's me, was going to do a quick run through and nail down the facts in a couple of days. Just the facts, Mam. I almost got my legs cut off. The magnitude of the claim should have warned me how desperate they were. One of the first stops an investigator usually makes is at the home of the family of the deceased, in this case, Liddy Berman. Now that would be the last place. No sense letting anyone know I was back in town. There would be no more parking tickets or ambushes by local reserve cops. The element of surprise was in my corner now and I intended to keep it there.

"Go to your place by the most indirect route. I don't want anyone to know we're back in town."

Connie made the exit and immediately doubled back under the highway.

"There's an access road that will take us past the town. We can double back and come in behind the hotel without anyone seeing us. I'll park a block away. How's that sound for a plan?"

"Not bad for a beginner. You might be a lot better at this than I thought. We'll have to put you on the payroll."

"Ten percent of six million sounds good to me."

"How about the whole six million, Connie?" She jammed on the brakes and came to a skidding halt.

"You wouldn't. That's criminal. It's...it's...It's grand theft - it's criminal just to suggest such a thing. You could go to jail for it and you have no right to involve me in something like that."

"Maybe...maybe not. Think about it this way. Someone decided Murry Berman was in the way. He might become a selectman, which meant the end of the good-old-boy system. So they took out a generous insurance policy and staged an automobile accident. That couldn't have been the work of just one person. There are industry checks to stop fraudulent acts like this. First, there is a line on the life insurance policy where the salesman swears an oath and signs an affidavit stating how long he's known the applicant and that the applicant is in perfect health. The medical form asks questions about the applicant's health and medical history. Both salesman and applicant sign affidavits testifying that it is all true. A special section for the wife testifies that the applicant is who he says he is and how long she's known him. So what if someone lies? The policy is null and void, the insurance company is responsible only for the return of the premiums paid to date."

"You really know your stuff, O'Keefe." The rain had stopped and the windshield wipers had changed their beat to a fleep-clunk, fleep-clunk cadence. Connie needed new wipers and this time they should be made in America.

"The applicant must go for a physical to a doctor of the company's choosing. If something is wrong, the policy is void. That can happen the day after the application or twenty years later. It can be tough. Say the old man passes away and the widow goes to collect on a $10,000 whole life policy they've been paying on for twenty-five years. She comes away with $50.00 because the old man borrowed against the cash value of the policy to pay a medical bill and never repaid the policy. Meanwhile, the company used their money for years and made an obscene profit giving nothing back to the old man and his wife. Or let's say that the salesman sold them a ten-year paid up life policy, so after paying excessively high rates for ten years, there are no premiums for the duration of the person's life. But they don't tell you that the face value decreases each year so that twenty-five years later, instead of ten grand, the widow gets only $139.10. There are worse examples but the point I'm making is, why would a company that cheats women, children, widows, and orphans, suddenly get generous and pay off a six million term life policy that should never have been written or approved? I'll tell you why, because somebody within the system approved it and stands to profit from the payment of that claim."

"But who has that much power?"

"That's what I intend to find out. The best way to do it is to steal the whole six million. That'll flush the bad guys out into the open."

"There must be other people with the same idea. How do you plan to get your grubby paws on the whole six million and what do you intend to do with it when you do?"

"I haven't figured it all out yet but I have some ideas. First of all, I have to track down some clues so I know who's involved. Myron Gates must have a pretty big share of the payoff to take such big chances. Lydia Berman would have to be very cold-hearted and uncaring to join in a scheme to eliminate her husband for money. I've seen cases like that but they were simple murder cases and there weren't as many people involved."

"So, the whole operation is rotten and you're going to snatch the prize to see who screams the loudest? That sounds a lot like what we used to do when we weren't sure which sow a little piglet belonged to on the farm. We'd grab the little bugger, who would start squealing, and watch to see which sow came running. Only problem was, sometimes she was too close for comfort, and you've never seen trouble, until you've had an angry sow chase you around the yard and over the fence."

"That's one I've never had to try, but it sounds exciting, and it could describe what will happen. Besides, if State Mutual is so determined to pay this claim, I owe it to Harry Dondi and myself to find out why."

"All right, I'm in but just make sure you let me know what happens when I come to my senses."

She put the car in gear and drove on. We parked one street away from the hotel and walked arm-in-arm along the back of the building to the sports center, which was really a swimming pool with some workout machines next to it. I followed Connie down several hall-ways to her apartment as she unlocked doors with her passkey.

"How long do you think it would take a crew of thieves to strip this hotel of all its furniture, room by room, Connie?"

"That's a weird question, Bill. Whatever makes you ask me that?"

"Oh, it's just the way I think. We came in here and no one saw us. You should put surveillance cameras on the back doors."

"Those are metal doors with high strength security locks and exit alarms. This place is like a fortress. No one gets in without a key."

"Happened to a 110 room hotel down in Tallahassee. Twelve moving vans cleaned the whole place out in forty-five minutes. Only ten rooms were rented that night, so they bypassed them, but six of the guests had their cars stolen and they all had alarms."

"I heard about that. They never found any of it and the night clerk heard nothing. That's hard to understand. How could that happen?"

"She was watching T.V., just like your night clerk, Shelly."

"Ok, what are you saying? Are you up to something?"

"From now on, Connie, we start doing things you may not like. There are ways of dealing with crooks like this. The law protects the criminal more than the victim. I don't go for that. The criminals I'm after are different. They work for a living. They have families and pay their bills, but they cheat, steal and thieve just like the muggers in the city parking lot, and sometimes they commit murder or violence against innocent people like Murry Berman. Before this night is out, I'm going to find out who's doing what in this town and I'm going to break a few laws doing it."

"Will you commit violence against anyone?"

"Only if I have to."

"I told you it was like a war in East Harbour. That was an intellectual statement. I didn't know what I was saying. Then, I watched you stand up like you were totally unafraid, and face that Jeep with the machine guns firing at you. You pointed that big gun of yours and fired it like you were doing target practice, only it wasn't really target practice, was it? Now, there are four dead men. I saw it happen and I still don't believe it. This is the big league, isn't it? We're playing for keeps and you love it." She started crying.

"Connie, if they left us alone, nothing would have happened. There'd be no six million dollar check. The state police and the Insurance Commissioner would have handled the investigation and we'd be out of it. Then Harry Dondi didn't listen to me and they gunned him down. I don't love the killing and the violence, I'm just good at it, and I couldn't live with myself if I let what they did to Harry go unanswered. Myron and his goons are going to be the sorriest bunch of bad guys this side of the Hudson River. They started it and I'll finish it."

"That's fine with me. I'm with you all the way. Where do we start?"

"I'm tired, hungry, and I smell. I need a shower, something to eat, and some sleep. I'll flip you for the shower."

"No need, you go first and I'll make something to eat."

The shower felt good and I let the hot water pound on my tired, aching muscles. The arm was starting to itch and I kept it dry like the Doc said. I put on a pair of shorts, a short sleeve shirt, and padded out into the living room to find Connie busy in the kitchen. She left the stove and walked past me.

"Keep an eye on the oven, will you? I'm going to shower and get comfortable." She went into the bathroom and I checked the oven. MMMMM, ravioli topped with cheese, one of my favorites, garlic bread on the counter, and a tossed salad in a bowl next to the bread.

I called Harry Dondi's personal line. Peggy Hughes, answered.

"Peggy, this is Bill O'Keefe. How's it going, Babe?"

"You should know, Bill. How do things get messed up like this?"

"Greed. Someone high up is pulling the strings on this one. Did Harry tell you anything about this case before he left the office yesterday?"

"He was excited, said you wouldn't believe it. He tried to get hold of you at Green's Marina, and when that didn't work, he went home to pick up some clothes and then he went to East Harbour. He said you were the best but even you didn't catch onto what was going on with the Berman case. He said it was the same thing all over again, only bigger, and when he blew the whistle, all hell was going to break loose. I don't know what he was talking about. You should have gone instead. He's not as good as you." I could hear her choking back the tears.

"Peggy, I'm sorry Harry got shot. I intend to find out who did it and I'll make sure they pay but it's complicated. Somebody tried to kill Harry and they ordered a hit on me this afternoon. They're going to a lot of trouble to cover their tracks."

"Somebody tried to kill you too, Bill? What happened?"

"Four of them are dead!"

"Oh no! Harry always said you were good. What's going on?"

"I need information to nail these people. Can you help me?"

"I'll do whatever I can, but are you working for the company now?

Did they agree to the 10%?"

"No, Peg, I'll be honest with you, I'm not. I'm doing this for Harry and I'm not getting paid. This one's on me and I need your help."

"Okay but I hope no one finds out. You're not too popular around here. Some people think you should be in the hospital instead of Harry."

"There's a lot going on that people don't know. They might think differently if they knew the facts. Like, for instance, why did Harry go to East Harbour after I told him to leave? Who knew he was coming here?"

"Two people knew: John Stanley and Frank Stillman. I don't know who else he told...probably his wife, Joannie. He called her before he left. Now they won't let her see Harry in the hospital."

"What do you mean, Peg? Why won't they let his family see him?"

"It's the police. They won't let anyone except the doctor and nurses in to see Harry. They said it's something about the murder investigation. It's horrible. A week ago, our lives were going along fine and then bang, everything blows up in our faces. If Harry...dies... oh God, if Harry doesn't make it, I don't know what I'll do."

"Take it easy, Peg. Harry won't die. He's a tough old bird." I waited again for her to stop sobbing.

"Tell me about the check, Peg. When are they going to issue the check to Lydia Berman?"

"That's tomorrow. John Stanley called Harry yesterday and told him to issue it Wednesday morning. He told Harry not to give it to anyone but Frank Stillman because he was the broker who wrote the policy. Frank is supposed to come in here at 5:00 PM and I'm to give him a check for six million dollars, payable to Lydia Berman. It's weird, Bill. Normally, in a case with such a big payment, one of the officials of the company would take it to the family, not some independent broker like Stillman, but those are John Stanley's orders right from Omaha. He called me again this morning to make sure I did what he wanted."

"Good old John, always following up on the details."

"He said something strange. He said you wouldn't bother anyone for a while. He said the state police had you in custody for murder and they suspected you shot Harry too, but of course you didn't."

"No! I was in Block Island on my boat and I can prove it. Harry's my friend. John Stanley is not to be trusted."

"I didn't think so, but I didn't say anything. Joannie said her son-in-law, Dr. Smith, talked to you and then he went to East Harbour and told Harry what you said. Dr. Smith is at the hospital now. He's the only one who can see Harry. They don't know he's related. What a mess."

"After I saw Dr. Smith, I went to Green's Marina and spent the day working on my boat. By the time I read Harry's notes, it was too late to call. I think you're right not to tell John Stanley anything about me. As a matter of fact, don't tell anyone I called. It could put you in a lot of danger. Don't trust Frank Stillman, either. There's one more thing I need, Peggy my love. I need the computer access codes."

"I can't help you there, Bill. Harry changed them all yesterday and he's the only one who knows what they are."

"Thanks, Peg. Now here's some advice. Stay out of East Harbour. Go to your mother's tonight. Don't go home and don't walk alone after dark. These are dangerous people and you know too much. Don't trust anyone connected with the company."

"Thanks for the warning, O'Keefe. I think I already figured the last one out myself. See you around, lover, and be careful yourself."

I hung up with more questions than before. I checked the ravioli in the oven and put the garlic bread in. Timing is everything in life. The bread should be ready just before the ravioli is served. My mind started turning over the questions in the Berman case. Why give the check to the very man who wrote the policy? Stillman should be fired for even writing the policy yet he was playing a central role in the payoff. Stanley should be looking for ways to stop that check instead of gloating over my arrest. Wait till he heard I was still free. If I didn't know him better, I'd wonder if he was involved but he didn't have the smarts to set up something this big. Someone else was involved. John never acted alone. I thought of Harry Dondi being guarded by the police. I looked up County Hospital and dialed the number. The operator answered and I asked for Dr. John Smith. She asked who was calling.

"Dr. O'Keefe from East Side Clinic. Would you page him, please?"
In less than a minute he came on the line.

"Dr. Smith here."

"John, this is Bill O'Keefe, what's going on there?"

"Bill, man, I'm glad to hear from you! Harry's still unconscious
and they're keeping him isolated. They won't let Joannie or Nicki in
to see him and they watch me like I'm a prisoner. Myron Gates was
just here telling everyone he was going to straighten everything out
and he keeps saying you shot Harry. Rumor is, you were wounded
in a shoot-out at your cottage. It's even on the news that they're
looking for you."

"John, there isn't much time. Get a full time night nurse in that
room with Harry. Don't let them kill him. They can't afford to let
him talk and they'll do whatever they have to in order to keep him
from telling what he knows. There's six million at stake here and
that's enough to make people do crazy things. We've seen some of
that already. Another thing, call Lt. Hank Gaines, state police," I gave
him the number, " and tell him I said he should take charge there
and get those local cops out of the hospital. Tell him I called but
you don't know where I am. You won't be lying because you don't
know. Tell Joannie I'm sorry about Harry. I was in Block Island when
I heard about it. I think she has enough intelligence to know I would
never hurt Harry for any reason. Tell her I'm going to straighten
things out. I'm back on the case and it's not for the money. She'll
know what I mean."

"She knows that, Bill. Just be careful. You're about the only hope
we've got. When will we hear from you again?"

"More likely you'll hear about me, John. Be careful yourself."

I checked the oven and was about to close it when I sensed a
movement behind me. Connie stood in the living room wearing one
of my shirts. It was unbuttoned and she was a vision of beauty. Her
hair hung wet down her neck to her shoulders, her breasts firm and
bold were held high and moved as she breathed.

"Do you think we can stop the clock for awhile, Mr. O'Keefe?"

I turned the oven off and opened the door. The ravioli could wait.

Then I went to her and slowly took her in my arms. She was eager and responsive. There was no preparation, no buildup, just an explosion of hidden passions too long denied for us both. I wanted this woman more than I ever wanted anyone in my life. That realization drove me to a greater and more intense effort, and I was rewarded with the passionate love of a woman who knew what she wanted and how to give it in return. We never made it to the bedroom and afterward we fell asleep exhausted on the couch in each other's arms oblivious of the evil surrounding us in the little hamlet of East Harbour. ❀

CHAPTER FOURTEEN

I awoke to the sound of dishes and the smell of food. Connie was setting the dining table, still dressed in nothing but my shirt. She came over to the couch and sat beside me. I marveled at the perfection of her body, the curve of her breasts, the slope of her hips, her long lithe legs. She was slightly tanned. The areas where her bathing suit had been were white, her skin soft and smooth, unblemished. It felt good to the touch. My own body was covered with scars from the past. I wanted to tell her how much some of those wounds had hurt, even after they healed. I wanted to tell her they didn't hurt any more, that I felt better, and I wanted it to stay that way.

"Sorry I woke you. I was trying to be quiet so you could sleep. You've had a hard day even for an iron man like you. Now that we've had our basic Freudian urges satisfied, how about lowering ourselves to the level of our survival instincts by indulging our appetites in some slightly overcooked ravioli, dried out garlic bread and soggy salad. The only thing still fresh and untainted is the wine. Want some?"

"Sure do, and after we taint the wine and ravage the ravioli, what say we reaffirm our faith in old Sigmund Fraud again."

"Only if you clean up your plate and help me wash the dishes."

"I'll do anything you ask, just don't leave me."

The food hit the spot and the wine went through me like a shot of morphine. I was conscious that I was having dinner in the presence of a naked woman with whom I'd just made love. This was a sort of connubial bliss I hadn't practiced for five years, and it had implications I wasn't really prepared for. I'd broken one of the cardinal rules of investigating. Willie Monk would have been all over me for this.

"Don't never fall in love durin' a case. It waters your brain and turns your legs to jelly and yuh can't dance in dat condition!" I don't know if Willie ever fell in love but maybe it was time to make my own rules. He would understand, especially under the circumstances.

"You have work to do, O'Keefe. I can see it in your eyes, so go get dressed and I'll clean up here."

I went to the bedroom and laid out my clothes and gear. I chose dark, loose fitting clothing with large pockets. It's hard to hide things, like guns and knives in tight fitting duds. I dressed and strapped on my war vest. It was designed around a shoulder holster for the .44 Magnum, which I wore on the left side, but I was without that weapon, having left it with trooper Rhodes back at the cottage. The image of that young trooper being dressed down by Hank Gaines for letting me escape brought a smile to my lips. I checked my tools on the right side of the vest: pliers, scissors, screwdrivers, probes, lock pics, flashlights- two sizes with extra batteries, a voltmeter, magnifying glasses and a lot more. Around the back were pockets loaded with a variety of useful items like coils of wire and rope, C-4 plastic explosive, flares, assorted knives starting with a small pocket type, and a Swiss army model with thirty-two different implements, a skinning knife, a switchblade and a small bolo acquired in Nicaragua on assignment with the army some years ago. Three small cameras, all had different lens and films, and on the left front, was a first aid kit, in case I got scratched. I put on a specially tailored, loose fitting, sports jacket that covered the whole vest. I strapped the 9mm Beretta with an extra clip, to my left ankle and the special services knife to my right ankle. My sneakers contained spring steel rods, which could be used for a variety of unmentionable activities. In my baseball cap was a pocket for a small .25 caliber automatic, a knife and a couple strips of C-4 explosive. Now, you're probably wondering what the hell I need with all this junk and how I'm able to carry so much weight. Without the .44 Magnum, the whole set up weighed 32 pounds. I found Connie dressed and the kitchen clean. She put her arms around me and a look of surprise spread across her face.

"You look bigger...What have you got under that jacket?" She opened it and looked at my vest.

"Just a few tools of the trade for a night out on the town. Gotta be prepared for whatever comes along. Are you ready to go?"

"Yes sir! Just let me get my coat." She wore dark blue slacks with matching shirt and sneakers. Her coat was a dark green. It was nearing nightfall and her outfit would blend in nicely. We walked to the back door of the health club, the reverse of the way we'd come in and continued to the next block, arm in arm, like two people out for an evening stroll. In the car I waited to see if anyone was tailing us.

"Take me as close as possible to the town hall without being seen. Be careful where you park or Myron will give us a $50 parking ticket."

"Don't worry. We'll come up behind the town hall and you can walk through to the back, but it's closed you know?"

She went down narrow streets lined with small houses, an occasional couple strolling on the sidewalks. No one seemed to notice us. A light breeze off Long Island Sound moved scattered clouds across a half moon giving the night a mysterious feeling. It was a perfect set up for a break-in and I intended to make the most of it. Connie stopped the car and turned the engine off. The darkness was not yet complete. The sky was still twilight, fading in the west behind us.

"Walk between those two houses," she pointed ahead and to the right. "The town hall is behind that big white three decker. The police station is to the right, so please be careful."

"Don't worry. This is an easy one. The hard part comes later."

I gave her a quick kiss and got out of the car before my hormones kicked in again. Walking very quickly, I avoided a street lamp on the corner by cutting through a front yard, across the street and between the two houses. A dog barked and a woman yelled, "Shut the hell up or..." The whole town was unhappy. A row of arborvitae separated the backyards of the houses from the town buildings. I stopped between two bushes and blended into the shadows. Floodlights cast an eerie light on the parking lot side of the town hall. The electric service for the town hall and police station came off the same pole in the front center of the parking lot. Two small telephone wires ran between the buildings. Maybe there was a fire alarm or a security system.

The back of the town hall was dark, shrouded in shadows. I walked casually across the fifty yards to the building and around the dark side to what was once the main entrance. The big double doors were ajar and I found myself in an entranceway with no alarms. This must have been the main entrance before the roads and parking lot were paved and the traffic shifted to the other end of the building. The locks were old. Not unusual in old municipal buildings. A door to the right led into a coatroom, now used for odds and ends like chairs, mops, brooms, and boxes, tops open with Christmas decorations spilling out. The double doors leading into the main building straight ahead were locked with a high quality dead bolt, very difficult to pick and impossible to break without lots of noise. Through a crack in the doors I could see a two-by-four barring the doors from the inside.

Back in the cloakroom, I found a door behind the stacked chairs. Its knob was removed but the plunger was still there. A screwdriver turned the spindle, disengaged the plunger and the door opened into the same assembly room I'd been in with Calvin Kinderhook. I moved carefully, checking for motion detectors but there were none. Across the hall the rooms marked "Town Offices" were locked. Sure enough, the town fathers were skinflints so they only had one flush toilet for the whole building and it wasn't locked. There was a connecting door inside with an old-fashioned lock made for a skeleton key.

It opened easily with a curved lock pick and I stepped into the Selectman's Offices, lined with filing cabinets, desks, telephones, artificial flowers and plants. The glare of the floodlights outside brightened the room, casting eerie shadows across the floor and furniture. A small red light, on a shelf, caught my attention. Sure enough, an intercom, its buttons set on speak made it an effective listening device. It was hard wired, not a transceiver type. The wire led outside. Someone, on duty in the police station would be aware of any noise from this room. Below the intercom on the next shelf was an aquarium with several exotic species of fish, the pump pushing bubbles up through the water catching the reflected light from the parking lot making an unusual iridescent scene within the tank. I carefully turned the volume knob to zero, lifted the intercom by its wire and let it sink slowly to the bottom of the aquarium: bubble, bubble...glub, glub, the little red light continued to glow, adding its own hue to the rest of the scene. I checked the police station for activity but no one came running across the parking lot, no police cars came screaming around the building...nothing. Well, so much for modern technology and high tech listening devices.

I quickly moved to the files and started a random search through each drawer and found a file marked "Stillman and Wallace: Insurance Contracts". They had the insurance policies on the town's business: employee health insurance, life insurance, retirement plans, liability, disability and accident coverage on town projects and contracts. This was big business. I was sitting on the floor below the windows, a small penlight held in my mouth when I spotted the insurance binders and bonding on the sewer project contracts. Everything, including the sewer disposal plant, was to be shared with two adjacent towns and came to over $80 million and the financing for the whole project was through one company, Credit Bonding and Assurity Company, 6639 Southwest Blvd, Chicago, Ill., the same address Willie and I had traced SARTXE payments to with the Credit Reporting Consultants, Inc. just three years earlier. The sums of money were huge and at the very end, was a 10% commission payable to SARTXE Corp. for consulting on the financing of the sewer project, to be paid through the financier, Credit Bonding and Assurity Company. That looked like an old-fashioned kickback.

Another file was marked, "Sewer Project". It had soil analysis reports, survey contracts, federally mandated surveys and studies. Then I found the Report of the Finance Committee re: proposed sewer project, Town of East Harbour. It had the same breakdown of monies as the other report. Next to the line that listed the 10% SARTXE consulting fee was a cryptic note, written in pencil in the margin, "Berman says not necessary-delete!" I was just about to read further when a car pull up outside. I quickly put the files back and shut the drawer just as someone unlocked the front door.

I hid behind a desk and waited. There was a rattling of keys unlocking a door and the lights went on in the next room. I moved quickly to the toilet door and across the hallway to the meeting room catching a glimpse of Calvin Kinderhook hanging his coat on a wall hook. He stepped over to a small table and spoke into an intercom.

"It's just me, Sam. I'll be here for a couple of hours. Let yah know when I'm finished."

"Okay, Mayor. All's quiet. Take your time," came the reply.

I went out the same way I came, retracing my way to the car.

"Good grief, O'Keefe! You scared me." Connie had been sleeping.

"Sorry I took so long. Looks like you put the time to good use. Enjoy your snooze?"

"Was I sleeping? Oh, no, tell me I wasn't asleep."

"All right, you weren't asleep. Now, let's get out of here."

"Where to, oh great master cat burglar?"

"I want to buy some insurance. Let's try Stillman and Wallace. I hear they have everything covered."

"They're just the other side of the center. Do you want me to go straight through the square or are we still trying to avoid detection?"

"Take it around the long way. Things will heat up fast enough without someone knowing we're here."

Connie drove through the back streets, observing stop signs and signaling her turns like she was a law-abiding citizen. She stopped beside a large two story white Victorian and pointed.

"That's it right there." A hand carved, wooden sign with 'Stillman and Wallace Insurance Agency', hung outside the second house down.

They'd done a nice job of fixing up an old house. It had aluminum siding, modern double glazed vinyl clad windows, metal clad fire resistant doors with modern locks and dead bolts. The cellar entrance was a modern steel double-doored unit with internal locks. A rather sophisticated alarm system with three green lights indicated separate internal alarm zones. I went around the house and found what I needed. Insurance brokers like a nice show but they all have one thing in common. They're cost conscious. If I wanted to be unkind, I'd say cheap. The windows on the second floor were original and the storm windows had been removed, probably because they needed repair. There were no screens and a nice old oak tree spread its limbs right next to the wrap-around porch on the side of the house.

A simple jump and a leg over, a jackknife and I was sitting on a large limb just below the porch roof level. I landed lightly on the roof and found myself looking into a window at the end of a hallway. I used a pair of polarized goggles and checked for light beams. No telltale light beams from motion sensors or noise detectors, no alarms on the glass. The multi-frequency debugger found no laser beams or infrared sensors. I was dealing with amateurs. A putty knife between the windows tripped the latch and I was inside.

A storeroom to the right yielded a copy machine, with file cabinets set up by year and name. No time to go through all of them. The secretary's office had file cabinets, computers and the coffee machine.

Across the hall, in the front of the house, was an office with plush leather chairs, a settee surrounding a massive executive style teak desk and a real Tiffany floor lamp. Mahogany paneling covered the walls floor to ceiling with bookcases to match on the three interior walls. Degrees and awards hung on the front wall behind the desk. A picture hanging just under a college diploma caught my eye in the reflected light of the street lamp. It was Frank Stillman, Rick Wallace and a third person I knew very well in front of a log cabin. Three deer hung from a tree limb. I knew the place. Only those who had a very special reason were invited to go to "The Lodge": people like the governor of the state, Paola Cantelli, presidents of corporations, princes and kings, senators. Even the President of the United States had been there. It was a hunting lodge in the mountains of

Idaho, owned by State Mutual and it wasn't for the casual use of the ordinary company salesman. Few people even knew of its existence. The fact that Stillman and Wallace were there with John Stanley was far more significant than anyone could imagine. Only deals of very great importance, worth millions, were made at "The Lodge". John wouldn't waste time, or reveal the existence of the place to anyone who couldn't deliver a deal of those proportions.

I knew this because I'd been there, undercover, trying to snag a senator who was about to launch an investigation of the insurance industry that might have resulted in very severe restrictions, if not outright regulation of companies and their business practices. We didn't succeed in convincing the good senator and he even turned down the call girl John offered him for the evening, saying he was a happily married man and didn't need the complications of a woman of the night in his life. I'd warned John but he always did know better. The senator left but never launched his investigation. He died of a heart attack two weeks later. I often wondered about John Stanley's luck.

A quick check of the room and desk brought pay dirt! Stillman was a computer fanatic and his entire business was on disk, sitting very conveniently on top of his desk in a small storage box next to a computer terminal. I was familiar with this type of computer, having worked with the same system for years in State Mutual. This one, just like the one on Rick Wallace's desk, would be on line with the State Mutual system in New York City. I found some formatted disks in the bottom drawer, fired it up and started copying. It took about five minutes and I had everything wrapped up. Stillman's entire business records were in my inside jacket pocket on six small diskettes. I did some exploring in the storage of the system, checking such words as "Murry" and "Berman", "Sewer Project" and "SARTXE" but found nothing. I was tempted to insert a computer virus just to be nasty, but I didn't want anyone to know I'd been there. I tried "Credit Bonding and Assurity" and got the entire file on the sewer project: payment schedules, dates and amounts, names of principals including SARTXE and it's 10% consulting fee with a P.O. box in Omaha this time instead of Chicago. There was a schedule of meetings, including one at "The Lodge" in Idaho the previous October. I selected another formatted diskette and copied the whole file. Nothing else came up on the computer but after I shut it down, I found the bottom right drawer of the desk locked.

What I found inside was worth the visit, a complete file on Murry Berman. Standard insurance policies on his life, house, car and family. A complete run-down and background report from a private detective including his finances, health history and school grades. There was a file from Murry's psychiatrist, a doctor Schwamm, in the city. It must have been stolen. On the fourth page was the doctor's diagnosis, Arachnophobia, and it was circled in red ink. A picture of Murry showed a wimpish looking man with bifocals, dark wavy hair, ears and nose too big for his face, and one side of his mouth sort of twisted up like he knew something you didn't. The last piece of paper in the folder was a list of names and monies. It sent chills through my body.

Lydia Berman	$1,000,000
Frank Stillman	1,000,000
Rick Wallace	1,000,000
Myron Gates	1,000,000
others	1,400,000
SARTXE	600,000
total	$6,000,000

Murry Berman had been murdered for his insurance policy. Another file on the bottom of the drawer was organized much the same. Two years before, Frank Stillman wrote a policy on one Alexander Bench in the amount of one million dollars. Same routine: the policy went through underwriting, was approved and issued without question. A report, on Alexander Bench, was provided by the same detective with a very detailed medical history and some notes about his work and habits. He was an architect. Death was by drowning and there was a picture of the check issued to his widow and beneficiary, Freda Bench. Then came the list of names and monies.

Freda Bench	$100,000
Frank Stillman	100,000
Rick Wallace	100,000
Myron Gates	100,000
others	500,000
SARTXE	100,000
total	$1,000,000

I took the files, stuffed them inside my shirt, left the same way I came and hit the ground walking. It was midnight straight up. "A good night's work, O'Keefe." I went around the back of the house, checking the street to see if anyone was watching. I walked through the backyards of the houses to the side street where Connie was parked. Before I emerged from the shadows of the last house, I stopped to check up and down the street. It was quiet...very quiet... and deserted! Connie's little Japanese sedan was gone. The street was covered with broken glass where she had been parked and one of her sneakers lay by the curb. ✻

CHAPTER FIFTEEN

My first impulse was to rush forward to the spot where Connie's car had been and pick up her shoe, but my instincts and training were screaming in my brain to retreat and cover my tail back through the yards where I'd just come. I should have known better than to leave Connie exposed like that. I didn't think anyone would suspect I was here in East Harbour. I'd underestimated Myron Gates, again. Now it was war. I checked the garden shed behind one of the houses and found a full can of gasoline. I took it to the side porch of Stillman's house, placed it behind a wicker chair in the corner, cut a good-sized chunk of C-4 explosive, buried a UHF detonator in it, and stuck the whole thing to the top of the gas can. So be it! If I had to, I would wipe out the whole damned nest with one big bang.

We learned our lessons in Vietnam. We never knew who the enemy was or where he would be, so we set charges everywhere, and when we left an area, Charlie would move back in. Then we pushed the button and everything went up, sort of like a doomsday bomb. Not very nice but extremely effective, and in a war zone, nice just doesn't cut it. East Harbour just became a war zone. Taking Connie wasn't nice. I walked to the center of town, worked my way around to the police station looking for her car. The dispatcher was watching TV.

I planted a C-4 charge inside the telephone service box. Then I went to the back of the building and climbed a service ladder to the roof where I'd spotted a transmitter tower. This was a communications center for the whole area with several lines leading to it. There was no tower on the firehouse so this one served both buildings. I set several explosive charges with UHF detonators and climbed down. The UHF detonators were more reliable than the FM type because they were less likely to be set off accidentally by a stray frequency. The ones I was using came by mail order from Hong Kong, but I'd had good luck with them. I tested them in the dunes around my cottage, setting them off with an actuator. The next target was a fuel tank behind the firehouse. No one ever thought of a terrorist attack when they put it there. I put an extra large charge on the tank next to the building. I could incapacitate the whole town with one push of the button.

I went back through the arborvitae and headed for the hotel, about a mile and a half walk, which gave me time to think. The vest felt a lot heavier and the lack of sleep and constant excitement of the day were starting to tell on my body and mind. Just 24 hours before, I was sitting in the cockpit of my yawl, Ginger at my side in total darkness, riding a nor'easter as the hull pounded its way through the night. Ginger was gone and now, less than a day later, I'd lost Connie as well. Letting two very beautiful women slip away in one day was embarrassing. Of course, Connie might have just given up, lost interest and gone home. Maybe she went to the bathroom and now she could be sitting in her car, dutifully waiting in that same spot. Women are like that. Maybe I should go back and check? 'No! Don't be stupid, O'Keefe...' The glass was from a car window and the shoe was bait. Someone was still back there waiting for you to walk out and pick it up.

I was tired, not feeling too great and my mind was doing funny things. It must have been fate. The good Lord looked down and saw that William Thackery O'Keefe was a man in need of some tender loving care, so he said "There's Ginger", but that didn't work out, so he said, "There's Connie, let's see how you and Connie get along."

So now life had added it's sick little twisted solution to that one and I had to find her and get her back. See? That wasn't hard to figure out. I cut through a yard and came to the back of the hotel. A fence separated me from the parking lot. I was exhausted and my arm hurt so I sat down and leaned up against the fence closing my eyes. A little voice said, "Let's face it, O'Keefe, you're not as young as you used to be." I told the little voice to shut up and get lost. My muscles were sore and my feet were numb. I willed it all to go away, and concentrated on my next move.

I stood up after a few minutes and felt the pain and exhaustion of the last few days settle into every muscle and bone of my tired, aching body. I'd been through this before and knew it would pass. I just had to keep moving. I managed to climb over the fence and landed behind two large dumpsters. Connie's car was parked at the other end of the building. Floodlights illuminated the whole lot and there wasn't another car in the area. I saw no sign of anyone, so I walked along the building, over to the car and looked in. The driver's side window was broken out but there was no blood. Her other shoe lay on the back seat. Her purse was on the floor in the front. There were no keys. Nothing is ever easy.

I left the purse and shoe in the car and went around to the side of the building to the back door of the kitchen. Back doors of kitchens are always open. I walked through the stockroom and looked around the corner. A boy was mopping the floor. I waited until he turned and walked casually through the kitchen, past the dishwasher, into the hallway and through the same door Connie had led me the first night. The office was open so I went in and checked Connie's desk for keys, but found none, so I went to Rick Wallace's desk. I found a 38-caliber revolver and put it in my jacket pocket. No sense in leaving a loaded gun around. There was a door to the left of the desk. I opened it a crack and could see across a hallway to Connie's apartment. A man with a double-barreled shotgun cradled in his arms stood at the end of the corridor. Lucky for me he was looking the other way. I closed the door and reviewed my options.

I was staring at the ceiling and got this bright idea. This was just your standard cheapo, put-it-up-fast-and-dirty hotel construction with dropped ceilings. I placed a chair on the desk and climbed up on it, lifted one of the 2'X4' ceiling tiles, looked up into the darkness above and got a face full of fiberglass particles, dust and other trash, along with a puff of hot air. Smart move, O'Keefe! I pointed my flashlight up into the darkness. There was a 4' space between the dropped ceiling and the second floor concrete slab above. The contractors buried eyebolts in the cement slabs to suspend the ceiling. Wires were attached to hang the ceiling and other necessary items, such as air conditioning/heating ducts, electric conduits, water, sewer, steam pipes, laundry chutes, and exhaust fans. I replaced the tile, wiped my eyes again, climbed down, and replaced the chair. No sense getting caught like a possum up a tree.

Shelves ran floor to ceiling around half the room. I climbed up these in the corner and pushed up a ceiling tile, being careful to turn my face away this time. I climbed through the hole onto the top of the corner wall. I got both knees on top of the wall, turned on the flashlight and replaced the ceiling tile. This type of construction was universally simple. Only one bearing wall existed, going up the center of the building with dividing walls running off it. The dividing walls, like the one I was on now, ran only up to the dropped ceiling and stopped, so I could crawl on top of them. They served their purpose, to separate rooms while all the utilities ran overhead, easily accessible for repairs.

I crept across a divider to what I thought was Connie's kitchen, carefully pulled up a tile and looked in. The kitchen was clear, but two men were playing cards at the dining table. That made three. I moved on, trying to be as quiet as possible but something made a noise to my right. I flashed the light over and came face to face with a big bull rat. He didn't look friendly so I stayed clear of him. So far I seemed to be getting away with this infiltration, but I had to face the facts as I moved around the bathroom and headed to Connie's bedroom. I was exhausted and weak from lack of food and rest. My arm was hurting more than ever.

'Count to ten very slowly, O'Keefe. Breath deep, pull up the ceiling tile and look into the bedroom. There's Connie tied up on her bed.' The bastards had tied her up. I pulled the tile up and scanned the room for more kidnappers, but she was alone. The door was open and the lights were off. I couldn't tell if she was asleep and I didn't want to startle her. I turned around so I could hold on to the cap of the wall and braced my feet against it. I started to let myself down and everything was going all right when suddenly, the wall fell apart in my hands and I came crashing down like Humpty Dumpty on top of Connie and the bed.

She came alive kicking and screaming and the more I tried to get loose and off the bed, the more entangled we became in the bedding and the ropes. I finally managed to roll over and fell out of bed. Connie landed right on top of me. I rolled over again to get her off my chest, so to speak, and stood up just in time to meet the first kidnapper as he came through the door, gun drawn and ready for trouble. He found it too because I was ready and hit him between the eyes with a right, taking his pistol out of his hand with my left. The second one wasn't so bold and stupid. He just stuck his head inside.

"What's goin..." I hit him with the pistol butt.

"God help us, O'Keefe. You sure have a funny way of entering a girl's bedroom." I untied her hands and loosed her feet.

"Couldn't help myself. When I saw you in bed, I just fell head over heals in love."

"They were on me before I knew what was happening," said Connie." I was awake, honest I was, but all of a sudden they broke the window and dragged me out of the car and off we went with Myron Gates driving a police car. Rick Wallace was waiting for me, here, and he helped tie me up. I couldn't believe he was in on it, but then I guess everyone in this lousy town is involved." There was resignation in her voice.

"Sounds about right." Someone knocked on the front door. "There's another guard outside. Quick, follow me." I went to the living room and pointed to a spot for Connie to stand about six feet from the door.

"Hey! Is everything all right in there? Hey!" He kept pounding.

"Yeh! It's okay," and I opened the door a couple of inches. "The bitch had to go to the toilet...come on in for a minute." He stepped into the room with the shotgun lowered just like I wanted him to.

Connie gave him a nice smile and cocked her hips a little just to keep his attention.

"Sorry, Roy, I had to go."

She smiled and I hit him as hard as I could with the butt of the pistol. I grabbed the shotgun as he went down and checked the hallway, closed the door and locked it. Roy had a .38 special in a belt holster and I took that too.

"Works every time. You know, we could start our own arms business. Just hang around your local police and pick up a few guns, then sell them to the highest bidder. What do you think, Connie?"

"I don't think that's legal."

"You're absolutely right, me lady, but what these guys are doing isn't exactly legal either and if you'll notice, they all have more firepower than any normal police force really needs. Help me tie them up."

The two men in the bedroom showed signs of coming around so I tied them up. I used a length of rope from the back of my vest to tie up the other one, and then dragged them all into the guest room where I spent my first night in town. I tied them to the bedposts, making certain that each one couldn't stand up. I did that by a sort of reverse hog tie, running a length of the rope from their neck to their feet. They could choke to death if they stood up. It's no joke being tied up like this, so maybe they would wonder if Connie suffered the same pain and discomfort. After a few hours of being tied up, the circulation is reduced to the point where the limbs become useless. Severe complications can set in and the person can lose an arm or leg. I would let these good old boys experience a dose of their own medicine.

"Which one of these upstanding citizens is Rick Wallace?"

"That one." Connie pointed to the first one I'd knocked out.

"Did they know I was in town?"

"No, they were gloating over the fact that you were supposed to be in custody and I was all alone. Honestly, Bill, I think they planned to kill me. They talked about some terrible things like they didn't seem to care. I could put them all in jail with what I heard. It was creepy."

"They've gotten away with a lot so far. Tell me what they said." We went into the living room and sat down. It felt good.

"They were talking about Murry Berman and how well things went, and something about how lucky they were they didn't have to do it another way. Then they talked about the payoff and how this would be the best one yet. Myron said he and the old lady could retire for good with one more like this one. Then Roy, that's the one outside with the shotgun, Roy Stillman, Frank's brother, asked who would take over when Myron left? Myron got really angry and told him not to worry because people with bigger and better brains could deal with those decisions. Then they had a nasty argument about what happened before. They forgot I was there. It got really confusing and I'm not sure what they meant."

"Take your time. Let's have a cup of coffee and relax." I went to the kitchen and put on the kettle.

Connie continued. "Roy Stillman said something about Myron messing up that deal with the Norman's three years ago, and how he almost got everyone put in jail, and it would have been the end of everything if his brother, Frank, hadn't stepped in and made the payoff to keep the widow quiet. Roy said that Myron should have learned his lesson when he got kicked out of the Navy for drowning that seaman. Good grief, I think they were talking about murder. I remember now, Myron was court martialed and dishonorably discharged from the Navy over the death of a seaman on leave in Baton Rouge. Myron was on the shore patrol.

"You say Myron was kicked out of the Navy? That's interesting. The man has a nasty history. The State Police still have an open case on that tourist. Norman, huh?"

"Yes, that's him, Norman. Someone called the F.B.I. when he disappeared. Then we didn't hear anything. Everyone acted like it never happened. Myron started yelling and Roy told him to shut up. Roy said any idiot knows you need a body to collect on an insurance policy. Then Myron said something about the chair thing...No! Let me think. He said something about the bench thing. Yes, something like, 'How did you like the way I did the bench thing? That's how you supply a corpse.' It sounded like they were talking about another murder. It was really scary. Then Roy told Myron to be careful before he put anybody down, because everyone was getting tired of doing the dirty work and taking the risks, while Myron sat on his fat behind and gave orders."

"I'll bet that caused trouble."

"It was weird. Myron just got real quiet and said they would take it up another time, and they shouldn't be talking about it with me in the car. Then he said not to worry, that there was enough for everyone and nobody would starve. Bill, it was really scary. I got the feeling Myron could be dangerous and maybe Roy Stillman might regret what he said."

"He'll regret it all right. This thing gets more interesting all the time but we have other problems. It's 2:00 A.M. and we're both exhausted. We can't leave those three unguarded. What say we take turns sleeping and guarding every two hours. That will take us up to 6:00 A.M. Someone will come to relieve these three jokers, sort of a changing of the guard. Myron hasn't learned about his four goons who died at the cottage yesterday. Hank's sitting on that. Someone will be looking for them and when it comes out they bought it, he'll be nervous, and he'll become even more dangerous."

"Is that possible?" Connie handed me a cup of black coffee.

"You bet it is. They don't know what happened at the cottage. Hank stalled them, but tomorrow he'll tell them about their four buddies. If Hank does his job, he'll take over guarding Harry Dondi, so by tomorrow afternoon, Myron Gates and Frank Stillman will be wondering if their plan is unraveling. They'll shoot first and ask questions later. I don't intend to be around when that happens...flip you for the first watch."

"I'll take it, Bill. You need the sleep. I'm too upset after being tied up."

"I'd like to tie you up sometime, Babe"

"When this is over, love, I'll carry a rope with me 24 hours a day."

"Deal! I've got a few knots I'd like to try on you."

I settled in on the couch and that was all I remembered until I awoke to the pounding on the door. I sat up and looked at the clock. It was 9:15 A.M. Connie was asleep on the chair across the room. So much for planning ahead. ❈

CHAPTER SIXTEEN

I ran to the spare bedroom. Our guests were still tied up. Closing the door, I went back to the living room, pulled my Beretta from its ankle holster, and looked through the security hole. There were three of them in street clothes. Hank was to the right with two troopers. Should I stay or run? I decided to open the door.

"Hello, Hank. Good to see you. Have a seat? Just made the coffee."

"Skip the coffee, O'Keefe. Geez, you look beat. Have a bad night?" He walked into the room casually, but the other two men spread out and started checking the place."

"I have three more for you in that bedroom over there. They're still alive but I don't think they'll move too fast when you turn them loose."

"Still alive, huh? What's wrong? You must be slipping or didn't you have time to kill them before we got here?"

"They kidnapped Connie last night. Myron Gates was in on it. When I got here they had her tied up in the bedroom."

"So, let me guess," Hank walked over and looked in the guest room. "You strolled in, tied them up, and saved the little lady."

"Something like that. If you'd like, we'll give you a statement."

"You gonna let me in on what's going on? Your boss, John Stanley, called the Governor again and demanded we put a stop to all the violence in East Harbour. Says he doesn't want his company, what's the name, State Something of Nebraska, yeh. He doesn't want them to get mixed up in any scandals. He asked where you were and how come he hasn't been kept up to date. Sorry, Bill, but I'm gonna need more than you've given me so far, or we're all gonna go in and have a long talk."

"Do you keep up on all the accidental deaths in the state, Hank?"

"Don't be silly. I can't even keep up on the murders in New York City let alone the accidental deaths throughout the whole state."

"How about unsolved murders and disappearances?"

"Are you trying to tell me something, O'Keefe?"

"Do you remember the disappearance of a man, last name of Norman, here in East Harbour about three years ago?"

"Do I? We had the F.B.I and everybody involved in that one. Suspected fowl play, insurance fraud and all sorts of things. Then the wife decides he probably just got tired of being married, and the insurance company didn't pay off, so it was dropped for lack of evidence." He looked at me closely. "Why? You know something I don't about the Norman disappearance?"

"Roy Stillman is tied to a bedpost in that room. He knows who did it and how much the widow got to shut her mouth. He's also responsible for the drowning death of an architect, Alexander Bench. There was a one million dollar insurance payoff. This is an insurance scam using murder and kidnapping involving a lot of people in this town. I don't know how they killed Murry Berman, but someone should be able to tell you."

"How did you find all this out in just one night?"

"If I tell you, the case against these people may fall apart. Besides, Hank, I need some time..."

"No way, O'Keefe! I'm in more trouble now than you can imagine. The Governor called me three times in the last 24 hours. The Governor, O'Keefe! He called me! If I let you go again, he'll have my head on a platter. Man, you gotta start doing things by the book. You can't just do whatever you want and the rest be damned.

You hearing me, buddy? The Governor is on my case. He wants you brought in before 5:00 P.M. today and no more questions." He turned to his two detectives, "Untie those three and get them out of here. We'll take them into headquarters. You, Miss Wilson, will come with us and make your statement. O'Keefe, you gotta come along too. I'm sorry but time's run out. Give me your gun."

I gave him my Beretta. "Hank, I'll go with you but do me a favor, will you? I need to go to the toilet. Man I'm in agony...just let me hit the head, wash my hands and face and I'll come along...Okay, Hank...Hank?"

"Sure...all right, Bill, but no games." He went with me to the bathroom and looked inside. "No windows. I guess you can't pull any of your smart assed-moves. Leave the door open." My vest lay on the floor next to the couch. No way I could take it with me.

"Hey, man, it's all right with me if you want the door open, but I gotta warn you, this is gonna to be a real stinker." I doubled over and held my stomach for emphasis. Connie turned her head so Hank couldn't see the smirk on her face.

"Okay, Okay. Close the damn door but don't lock it."

"Thanks, Hank. I owe you one. I'll only be a few minutes."

I gave Connie one last look and she threw me a kiss. I turned on the hot water, flushed the toilet a couple of times, waited for the mirror over the sink to fog up and wrote on it. Hank would know what it meant: PHONG PHO, our objective off the map during a mission in Vietnam. Every time we made a move, the VC pounced on us. It was like they knew our every move before we made it. Finally, I took Hank aside and told him my thoughts. There was a leak. No one else knew about our mission. The way things were going here, I was certain there was a conspiracy at the highest level of State Mutual and the Governor was now involved in it. The tip-off was the 5:00 P.M. deadline. I did a couple more flushes, stood on the toilet seat, pushed out a ceiling tile, climbed up into the utility space, and retraced my route just as I'd done the night before, replacing the ceiling tiles as I went.

I crossed the ignition wires on Connie's car and took off. This put Hank in a bad spot but I had to stop Myron Gates and Frank

Stillman. They might get away with their fraudulent scheme and I would end up in a lengthy legal entanglement. There is no real justice in the world.

I found the fastest, most direct route out of town to the main highway, Route 25, and followed it east to Mattituck, connected with Middle Road and drove to my turnoff. It was a beautiful morning with scattered puffy clouds dotting a clear blue sky, the sun full and climbing to its daily zenith in the heavens. A fresh ocean breeze gave a clean, crisp smell and the promise of a warm summer day. Nice day for a sail on the Sound if you're not an insurance investigator wanted by the police as a material witness in a multiple murder investigation involving half a town, millions of dollars and one of the largest insurance companies in the world. Willie Monk used to say it better than anyone.

"You know somethin, O'Keefe?" He used to say. "When you're a insurance investigator, yah don't hafta go huntin no trouble. All yah gotta do is say your name and trouble comes to ya like a bulldog chasin a rat up a sewer pipe."

That's how I was feeling. If Hank didn't get me, Myron or one of his goons would try their best to take me out. I had to start moving on them. I needed something they weren't expecting, but first I needed a change of clothes, a good meal, a hot shower, and a good firearm since all mine had been confiscated by the state police. Who needs gun control?

I drove Connie's small compact right up to the cottage and parked it between two large sand dunes, where it was hidden from both the road and the beach. The Nature Conservancy Beach Watch Committee could go pound sand. No pun intended. I had more important things on my mind than environmental issues. The Jeep was gone but the cottage was still a mess, so I spent a few minutes straightening up. The solar hot water supply, a fifty-gallon holding tank, was up to temp so I took a nice hot shower, dried off, and changed to a clean set of duds. I retrieved my service issue Colt .45 with five spare clips from the safe. It was old, the barrel worn, making it inaccurate. It was heavy and loud, but this was war, and I had no other weapons that carried the necessary firepower. If you're going to a dance, you wear the proper shoes or you can't do the steps when the music plays. The Colt made things proper. I took the spare remote control actuator from the desk drawer. My other one was in my vest back at Connie's place. I tossed the weapon and clips into a tote bag and headed for the door. 'Hey Myron, here I come, ready or not'.

Just as I stepped out the door I ran into Milt Neddleman, the president of the Nature Conservancy Committee. He was breathing fire.

"Mr. O'Keefe, we've been very patient with you over the years but this is too much. Burning vehicles are not allowed. You will explain or we will start proceedings to have you removed from the refuge."

"I can't stop and chat, Milt. I'm really sorry about the burning Jeep, but those fellows were breaking the rules and I just got so mad that I lost it and I took my gun and blew up their Jeep. They'll never trespass again, you can bet on that." I adopted his style of speech to make myself more convincing."

"My God, man. You don't have to shoot people. There's the law, you know."

"Yeh, well, Milt. You know I don't have a telephone, your rules, so I had to act sort of on the spur of the moment."

We chatted a few more minutes and I promised to be more careful next time and to stop shooting people. He left and I took the Caddy, headed west, stopped at a Burger Hut and picked up an order to go: three Burger Bangers (hamburgers with everything), two Sly Fry (small French fries), a Black Calf (small chocolate shake), two Isaac Newton's (hot apple pies), and a Columbian Chaser (small cup of coffee). I'd pay a heavy price later when all that stuff hit the old innards, but by then I'd be dead, in jail, or a free man without a care in the world. It was nearing noon and traffic on the Middle Road was picking up. The ferry from Orient Point docks every hour. These people are in a hurry to get someplace and they pay the extra toll to cut across Long Island Sound. I found myself in the middle of a group just off the ferry.

I was munching on a dried out Burger Banger and thinking about Connie and what it would be like to have her in my life. The road was two-lane asphalt, with a small dirt breakdown lane and a strip of grass extending along beside the road and down to a drainage ditch. Beyond that were either trees or fields. Most of that area of Long Island is farmland and picturesque countryside.

Two cars were ahead of me and one behind. We were traveling about 45 mph with plenty of space between us. No one seemed in a hurry. The lead car was driven by an older man, his wife beside him, no doubt telling him what to do because every now and then she would point at something and start talking and he would slow down to 30-35 mph, and we all did the same until she stopped pointing and talking, and then he would speed up again. The fellow following them, just ahead of me, must have been a local, because he didn't seem to mind and I was on my third hamburger and second fry so I was content to go along with the flow. Directly behind me, however, was one of those Travel-alls, a big monstrosity of a house on wheels that you see parked in somebody's yard with a "For Sale" sign. Then two weeks out of the year, mom and pop dust it off, take out a loan, fill up the gas tanks, pile the kids in back, the boat and deck chairs on top, and the V.W. on a tow bar behind.

Well, this fellow must have been having trouble keeping it in gear, because every time mom and pop slowed down, dad in the prairie schooner started honking his horn, shaking his fist, and weaving all over the road. I thought about pulling over so the whole damn caravan could go on its merry way, when a small truck came up behind the Travel-all and tried to pass. It was one of those foreign built pickups, modified for off-road use with four great big monster tires and the body raised up real high so the chassis don't drag in the swamp and the alligators won't bite your butt. It had those chrome roll bars up on top, chrome radiator guards, chrome running boards, a big aerial sticking up off its tail with a flag, and dual stacks up the backside of the cab just like the big guys, and guess what? It was black.

So here's the picture. This jerk in the black 4X4 tried to pass the dad in the Travel-all, mom and pop up front got into it about that time and slowed down to 30 mph, a line of cars was coming from the other direction, and I was just biting into a hot Isaac Newton, which is what I consider one of the few real enjoyments in this life. So you would think that with all that going on, especially, with the on-coming traffic, the driver of the little black truck would think twice before pulling out to pass? But no! There he was, making his move. Dad, in the Travel-all was honking his horn and shaking his fist, weaving all over the road, but when the black truck started around him, he sped up so the truck couldn't get back into the lane. If that wasn't enough, he tried to bump the truck off the road. So help me, he swerved left and tried to bump that black little 4X4 truck off the road. I was mildly amused by what was going on behind me and a bit concerned for my safety. The truck got the message and pulled back letting the oncoming traffic pass, so I started in on my other hot Isaac Newton and added the Columbian Chaser to wash it down. Then it all started over again.

Another clump of cars appeared coming at us around a bend. Ma pointed and pa slowed down. The guy ahead of me slowed down, the Travel-All dad started honking his horn and shaking his fist, the Japanese 4X4 started to pass, and it dawned on me that I was witnessing something weird and maybe I was the target.

Two guys in the back of the pickup suddenly stood up with shot-guns. They had hoods over their heads, like ski masks with eyes, ears, and the mouth cut out. I was watching in my rear view mirror and the fellow in front of me must have been doing the same because he wasn't looking ahead. He suddenly jammed on his breaks to avoid hitting mom and pop. I did the same, the black pickup came up beside the Travel-All and the guys in the back started shooting. One fired into the Travel-All and the other fired at me, blowing out my rear window. I have to give the dad in the Travel-all credit. He stayed right in there and didn't even flinch. He must have been from Jersey or maybe he just watched a lot of T.V. Then again, there was the familiar little red disk on his front bumper that said, Simper Fi, ex marine! Whatever it was, he hung in there while all hell broke loose. He didn't give an inch. Instead he wheeled a hard left, banged into the truck, and sent it out of control, across the highway, into the drainage ditch and through a fence. One of the shooters went flying over the tailgate into the drainage ditch with his shotgun still in hand. Oncoming traffic became an oncoming pile-up of wreckage as cars spun out, hitting each other ramming into everything. I managed to get over to the right onto the grass and stopped the Caddy in time to witness cars crossing each other and spinning into the ditches on both sides of the road. The Travel-all pulled over just ahead of me. The guy in front of me was sandwiched between the wreckage of two cars in the opposite lane, and the cause of it all, mom and pop, were still going up the road, untouched by it all: mom still pointing and yapping as pop slowed down and sped up totally unaware of the destruction they just left behind.

I got out of the Caddy just in time to see the 4X4 turning around in the field and the fellow with the shotgun coming up out of the ditch. I didn't have my .44 magnum with its long distance capability, and I didn't have the 9mm Beretta with its smooth recoil, superb action and extra loads. All I had was the old heavy U.S. Army issue 1911A Colt .45 with seven shot clips and a worn out barrel. I grabbed the tote bag, set it on the hood of the Caddy, chambered a round, and turned to face the shotgun. He fired first and I could hear..."No!" I could feel the buckshot snap through the air beside my face. It was too close. I stepped forward, leveled the Colt and with both hands commenced firing. People all around were screaming in terror and running for cover. The fellow with the shotgun in the ditch disappeared and there was no doubt in my mind that he was dead, but now I had another problem.

The truck came across the field, through the fence and across the ditch straight at me. They ran over their own buddy without stopping. I loaded another clip and commenced firing, hoping to hit the driver or the shooter in the passenger side, but the truck just kept on coming. I grabbed another clip, rolled left, and hit the pavement as they came past going down into the other ditch. The shooter in the back of the truck cut loose with a couple of rounds but the bouncing truck spoiled his aim. Then the driver made a mistake. He jammed on his brakes and the shooter in the back went sprawling down into the bed of the truck. This gave me time to load another clip and when I came up they were sitting ducks. The truck was barely moving and it presented a choice target. I went for the driver and passenger and then the masked shot-gunner in back. The shot-gunner fell over the side into the ditch and didn't move. The truck continued to move very slowly into the field beyond. The right door opened and a man, holding his side, stepped out and fell face down while the little black 4X4 began a slow wide turn around the field, its driver slumped over the wheel.

I reloaded the Colt. Drops of blood were hitting the pavement next to my feet. I wiped my forehead and found the source. That first blast of buckshot had been closer than I realized. People were gathering around me so I walked down into the ditch to the shot-gunner and rolled him over. I found a black pouch containing a badge and a picture I.D. of Sergeant Samuel Gates, East Harbour Police. Nothing like keeping it in the family. Dad from the Travel-All came running down the grassy slope. He was middle aged, fat and bald with an aggressive take-charge air. Three stripes decorated his hat.

"Man! That was some shootin friend. My hat's off to you. Not many guys can handle a service issue Colt like that. You a cop or somethin?"

I looked out across the field at the little black truck, which had finally stalled up against a tree and handed the I.D. to the dad.

"Take over here, Seargent..." and then as I walked away I yelled over my shoulder. "Simper Fi!"

He turned to me with his clenched fist held high and yelled, "Hooraaaah! Simper Fi!" ✺

CHAPTER SEVENTEEN

Broken glass covered the inside of the car. I brushed it off the seat, started the engine and got out of there, picking my way past wrecked vehicles and injured people, trying to control the shaking in my hands. After a few miles, I realized it wasn't my hands that were shaking. It was my whole body, so I concentrated on that and had better luck. I drove past the East Harbour turnoff, said a silent prayer for the widows and orphans of the men who had just died, and kept going until I saw the familiar little blue sign with the "H" and an arrow pointing to the exit ramp. I was still bleeding but I could see in the rearview mirror that it was just a crease on my upper right forehead, so I held a Burger Hut napkin against it as I drove. My mother always said head wounds bleed a lot because the heart pumps more blood to the head to keep the brain supplied with oxygen. My father said that since his son, that's me, had no brains, I would never have to worry about bleeding to death from a head wound. He might have changed his mind if he saw this one. At the Emergency room of County Hospital, the receptionist was frantic trying to find anyone who knew how to deal with a man bleeding all over his head, face, neck, shirt, and pants, a Colt .45 in his belt, and was still walking and talking as if nothing was wrong.

"Right in here, sir! Please...ah...sit here and I'll get somebody...

ah just sit there." She pointed to the stretcher table, pulled the curtain and rushed off. Well, that's it folks. She'd done her job. Got the bloody oaf out of the reception area where he might offend someone. We don't like real blood and violence. It's all right on T.V. or in movies, but not in real life. So, there I was out of sight for the moment but not for long. I considered bleeding all over everything just to show them but then I remembered it was my blood. I was becoming giddy. Had to watch it. Too tired, loss of blood, stress reaction. Still had work to do. Got to talk to Harry Dondi and get to the payoff.

The receptionist turned up with a nurse in tow.

"Oh, my, Annie said she had a bleeder. Let me see what we have..." She was a brunette with all the right stuff in the right places. She opened a drawer in a side stand and picked out some gauze patches and alcohol rubs.

I'll clean you up but we must wait for doctor to look at this and decide what needs to be done. I think you'll need some stitches but that's up to doctor." She gently rubbed the blood off my neck and face while holding a double gauze patch to the wound.

"Do you have a doctor on staff here at the hospital?"

"Yes, Dr. John Smith. I don't know if he's on staff but I think he's been around the last few days."

"Oh, yes...Dr. Smith. He's been upstairs with that poor man they found shot out on the highway. Just hold this pad on the cut and I'll call him. By the way, how did this happen?" She picked up the phone but I caught the edge in her voice.

"Gun shot."

"What?"

"Gun shot. Fella tried to shoot me with a shotgun."

"I see, and what happened to him?"

"Dead! I shot him back."

"I see. I'll be right back." She put the phone down and left me holding the gauze pad to my head. I picked up the telephone and dialed "O" for operator. It rang three times.

"Yes, may I help you?"

"Operator this is Doctor O'Keefe in Emergency. Please page Dr.

John Smith. I'm at extension 4302." In less than a minute the phone rang.

"Dr. O'Keefe here."

"You show up in the damnedest places. What's up?" I told him and he said he'd be right there. He showed up in less than a minute.

"Hello, Bill," He shut the curtain behind him.

"Nurse Jones was about to call the police when I came down. I told her I'd handle it." He started examining my head.

"Thanks. How's Harry doing?"

"He's awake and talking. You were right about the local police. Your friend, Lt. Gaines, wasted no time getting down here with a couple of his men. Myron Gates, put up a real stink, but when Lt. Gaines showed him the Governor's signed orders and a court order to back it up, Myron left in a huff. I don't trust him though."

"What's Harry have to say about who shot him?"

"Well, Harry did what you suggested. He was leaving East Harbour to go back to his office to stop payment of the insurance claim on Murry Berman's death. He looked at the medical application on the policy and compared it with the police report and the coroner's report, and he saw the discrepancies just like you said. Berman wore glasses. He was even partially blind in his right eye. Whoever took that physical, had 20-20 vision and didn't wear glasses. Murry was a small man. He weighed 145 pounds and was 5'4". The guy who took the physical was 200 pounds and over 6'. Also, there was the thing about the excess adrenaline in Murry's system." He cleaned the wound and started stitching. It hurt.

"The curious thing about all this," I said, "is the way the policy was processed. No insurance company writes double indemnity clauses anymore. Yet this policy was written and approved in record time, and the only people who get targeted are Harry and me and we're the good guys." Dr. Smith finished stitching, took a pair of scissors and clipped the ends of the threads.

"You're saying something is rotten somewhere in the system?"

"There's evidence this isn't the first murder for profit scheme in East Harbour." I told him everything.

"Sounds like you've been busy, O'Keefe. Now, take off your shirt and let me look at your arm." Before I knew it, he'd swabbed the cut on the back of my arm with alcohol and started pulling the stitches. It stung.

"It doesn't pull as much anymore. Feels a lot better. Thanks Doc. Hey, can we go up and see Harry? I have some ideas he might like to hear."

"Sounds all right to me but we'll have to run through security. What's your status now, O'Keefe? You still a wanted man?"

"Yeh, maybe you could find me an outfit that isn't so messed up so I can blend in better. Oh, by the way. There was a hell of a pileup out there. The Emergency ward is going to be very busy soon."

"I'll check to make sure they're ready and then we'll go upstairs."

We left the Emergency Room and rode the elevator up to the second floor, stopped in a doctor's lounge and picked up an operating outfit, you know, the light green shirt and pants? There was no trouble walking through doors after that. It was "good afternoon, Doctor" and "how are you Doctor?" and "how'd it go Doc?" We went to Intensive Care on the third floor and found Harry Dondi awake and talking, tubes and needles sticking out of him all over. There was a guard inside the door with his back turned as we walked in. It was trooper Philip Rhodes. I said hello.

"Well, well, well...Mr. O'Keefe! You caused me a good deal of trouble, sir." He wore plain clothes and his hand was under his jacket. He was debating about what to do when Dr. Smith stepped between us.

"Philip, he's here to see Harry. I'll take responsibility."

"I don't think so, Doc. Lt. Gaines said nobody, and that means nobody outside the immediate family is to get in here." He pulled his gun, a S&W .357, and pointed it at me about waist high. I didn't move.

"Now, there's no need for that," said Harry. "He's Okay, Phil, let him in. That's my old friend I was telling you about. "Phil stepped back and waved us in but he didn't holster his weapon. I went to Harry's bedside, conscious of the gun pointed at my back.

"O'Keefe, you old dog! You were right about everything. I should never have gone to East Harbour. They got me when I came onto the main highway. There were four of 'em in a little black pickup truck. Never saw them coming. They just showed up beside me and started blasting away, two of 'em in the back with shotguns and one in the front with a pistol. Damn! It was like the 4th of July. They just drove by, blasted me, and drove off. I got my car stopped and that's all I remember. I guess I crawled out of the car because they said I was in the ditch." His voice grew weaker and I could tell he was living it over again.

"Did the truck have real big tires and a chromed roll bar with dual stacks?" I asked looking straight at trooper Rhodes.

"Yah! Geez, Bill, come to think of it, you're right, it did...Hey, how'd you know about that?"

"They won't be shooting at anyone again...ever."

"You mean they're dead?" asked Harry.

"Yes, Harry, and three more were taken into custody this morning, four are dead out in the sand dunes, and three more permanently injured in the parking lot at the Daylight Inn just six days ago. That's fourteen so far and you started it all."

"Me? How the hell did I start it? I didn't do anything wrong." He looked hurt.

"That's just the point. You did what you should have done. You called me and I went to work. Only we didn't realize how big this thing was. The policy on Murry's life was approved and issued right under your nose. Then the notification of claim was delayed in-house so you had no time to investigate. You called John Stanley, he unloaded on you and you panicked. It was Friday afternoon and you knew time had run out. Stanley was going to hang the whole thing on you, so you did what he didn't expect by calling me, and I did what he least expected. I went to work for State Mutual again, something both Willie Monk and I swore we'd never do. I did it for you, Harry, because we're buddies and buddies don't ever let buddies go with their backsides unprotected."

"And that's why John said the Board refused to pay your 10%, because he knew you'd quit and the claim would be paid."

"Right again, Harry, and when you went to East Harbour and

started poking around, you just stirred up a hornet's nest of paranoia among the conspirators of this whole fraudulent scheme."

"But, Bill! There must be dozens of them involved in this scheme. How can there possibly be so many people in one town involved in murder and insurance fraud and the police don't know about it?"

"Because, Harry, the East Harbour Police are the ones who are shooting at us." I looked at trooper Rhodes and saw he'd lowered his weapon. He opened his jacket and returned it to its holster.

"Are you kidding? Why would the police in a small town start shooting at innocent people? We never did anything to the Police."

"We're not innocent people. We're insurance investigators. They controlled East Harbour at one time. They sold land, built houses, levied taxes and got rich; at least for them it was getting rich. Then, East Harbour became a bedroom community for commuters and the houses the locals built were bought up by yuppies with different values. The newcomers didn't believe it was right for all the locals to be on the town's payroll. They wanted competitive bidding on town contracts. They wanted to reduce the number of locals on the town's payroll. They passed zoning laws restricting development on land owned by the old timers, and that literally put some of them into bankruptcy. Murry chaired the town finance committee. That meant he was at the head of the yuppies' efforts to make all those changes. He was thinking of running for selectman and that would have made him one of the three bosses of the town's employees, which was unacceptable to the locals."

"So, they knocked him off?"

"Well, actually, they were more creative. First, they took out a very large insurance policy with double indemnity on his life. Then, they must have knocked him off, but I don't know how they did it. I have an idea but I can't prove it as long as I'm running around like a fugitive. Normally, insurance investigators work out in the open where we just ask people questions."

"In East Harbour if you ask questions, someone starts shooting at you," said Harry.

"The other thing is, Murry may not have been murdered. Maybe his death was just a real lucky break. Or maybe he was on to something else. Harry, have you ever heard of a company out of Chicago named SARTXE?"

"No, I can't say I have. What's that got to do with Murry Berman?"

"Don't know for sure, maybe nothing, maybe everything. Whatever happened, it seems a lot of people wanted him out of the way."

Harry said, "Those computer runs you requested turned up an interesting fact. There's a Thelma Wallace working in underwriting. She's is Rick Wallace's sister. She didn't tell anyone when she was hired and since there are no more security checks, she was never uncovered. Normally, relatives are not allowed to work within the company."

"So, she filed the policy and sat on it until the last minute?"

"But how could she have gotten the policy approved?" asked Dr. Smith.

"Easy. No one signs their own name anymore. They use stamps. Each underwriter is supposed to it keep locked up in a desk drawer. Each underwriter makes a stamp of their signature when they get the job. Obviously, someone left one of these lying around and Thelma Wallace used it to approve Murry Berman's policy."

"It's simpler than that," said Harry. "The underwriters just hand their stamps to a clerk like Thelma with a stack of policies and she does the approvals. It's part of the new efficiency campaign launched last year. Cuts down on office expense."

"That would never have happened when Willie Monk was there. That's an obvious invitation to fraud."

"Cost efficiency is the thing now. The company thinks the money lost to fraud is so little, it doesn't justify all the controls."

"Is six million dollars worth tracking down? Someone should have fired Frank Stillman for writing that policy, and John Stanley should have backed you for the 10%. This thing goes higher than you think, Harry."

"John Stanley? No way, Bill! He would never sabotage his own company. It just doesn't make sense." He was getting upset.

"It makes perfect sense. No one can prove anything. The company won't prosecute. The local police have the car and they won't prosecute. The grieving widow is in on it. Half the town will be paid off for participating in the cover up so that leaves you and me, Harry."

"So, what can we do?" asked Harry.

"I need some information. Give me the access codes to the computer system. I could hack them out but there isn't time. Peggy says you have them."

"Oh, wow, I don't know about that. Geez, Bill, if they ever found out, I'd be fired."

"Oh, come on, Harry, fired? These people tried to murder you and you're worried about being fired? Think man! Who the hell knew you were in East Harbour? Who did you tell?"

"Damn it, O'Keefe! I know what you're driving at. I told John Stanley I was going to East Harbour and that I was going to stop the payoff. I can't believe he had anything to do with this, but you're right. No one else but Connie Wilson knew and she didn't tell anyone."

"That's right, Harry. John Stanley is the one who tipped them off and almost got you killed. Now, what are the codes? I don't have much time before Frank Stillman picks up the check, and it's all over once the funds are dispersed. We'll never prove anything."

I got what I wanted from Harry. He was like a man who just realized his best friend had betrayed him. The only thing worse would have been to find out his wife was cheating on him. He gave me the codes. I thanked him and said goodbye.

Trooper Rhodes met me in the hallway as I was leaving. "I just talked to Lt. Gaines. He said you can go as long as it's still before 5:00P.M." I left the green operating duds with Dr. Smith at the elevator, rode down to the ground floor, and went out through the Emergency ward. This time I didn't cause a sensation. The place was jammed with the injured from the accident on the highway. I was just another ambulatory case. That is, no one noticed until I stepped outside. They were waiting for me, and this time it was well planned.

Two of them stuck shotguns in my back. Four more were hiding behind two pickup trucks. Two flankers on either side closed the circle with riot guns. Myron waited until it was safe to step out from behind one of the trucks. I liked the odds except for the riot guns. I could probably move fast enough to avoid being hit if everyone was using a handgun, but not with two riot guns in my back and two more on either side. Of course they were all pointing their guns at each other, but that was academic. There was no sense in causing a blood bath with me in the middle, so I raised my hands very slowly and stood still.

"Well, Mr. O'Keefe. We meet again. How did we do this time?" Myron Gates strutted his 250 pound butt around the circle like a peacock on a warm spring morning.

"You did just fine, Myron. Not bad for a bunch of country hicks. You finally got it right." I smiled to make him think I was still friendly. ❊

CHAPTER EIGHTEEN

"Being captured by the enemy isn't the worst thing that can happen." My commanding officer said that to everyone who arrived at the unit in Vietnam.

"Even getting killed by the enemy is not the worst thing that will ever happen to you. The worst thing that will happen to you is getting yourself captured and not escaping, because," he said, "if I ever find you and you haven't escaped, I'll torture you worse than the enemy ever will."

We laughed at that speech but after spending a tour of duty under Captain Oswald Matthew Thornton from Mesquite, Texas, nothing was a laughing matter. More than one captured recruit escaped with Captain Thornton's words in mind. Right at the moment, I had in mind to just stay alive. Myron had me cold turkey. I couldn't try an escape until things changed. They took the Colt .45 and extra clip but they missed the Special Forces knife on my left ankle. Myron took the keys to my Caddy and gave them to one of his boys.

"Todd, take that Caddy and follow us. I don't want nobody findin nothin after this." Very articulate that Myron.

The backseat of the police car was littered with cigarette butts, candy wrappers, banana peels, and piles of Burger Hut garbage. The man was a junk food junkie as well as a first class creep and a murderer. In the front seat was one of the men with a riot gun and he kept it pointed at me through a small square hole in the wire mesh barrier between the seats. Not much I could do with my hands cuffed behind me, the riot gun pointed at me, and everyone watching me, so I sat back and listened to the chitchat. Myron was very proud of himself.

"You give us a merry chase, Mr. O'Keefe, but we kept on yah till we gotcha. I gotta say, man, you are the hardest fella I ever did see to kill. We done everything possible to put you away and still you ain't dead...right, Billy? Am I right?" He nudged the other fellow's arm.

"You're right, Myron. But we're gonna change all that now."

"Yah! Ha, ha, ha, ha." Myron laughed like a cackling hen. More like a cluck than a cackle. Sounded like a man with a hietal hernia. Fat people often develop those and it makes it difficult for them to laugh, sneeze, cough, or hiccup. I once heard about a fat man who hiccupped himself to death. He literally sprung a leak and died of internal hemorrhaging. I silently hoped that would happen to Myron, but he didn't deserve such an easy death. I had a better plan for him. He just didn't know it yet.

"You're awful quiet back there, boy! Hey, you...O'Keefe! I'm talkin to you, son! You answer me when I talk to you or I'll teach you a lesson. You understand me, boy?"

"You shouldn't get yourself too excited, Myron." I shifted to my right where I could see the side of his face. It made it more difficult for Billy to hold his riot gun on me. I wanted to watch Myron's eyes. I wanted to know how far I could push the fat bastard.

"You tellin me what to do, son? You tryin to tell me to calm down right? But you really tryin to get me riled! That what you doin, boy?"

"Yeh, Myron, I'm trying to get your goat. You know what I mean, you fat slob!"

He jammed on the brakes so hard I was thrown against the front seat. Billy disappeared under the front dash and the shotgun discharged as he went down. Fortunately, the muzzle of the gun was pointed up and to the left so the charge of "OO" buckshot went through the roof above Myron's head. The sound of the blast was deafening. I pushed myself back up on the rear seat into the right hand corner. Myron was leaning over the steering wheel, his eyes closed, holding his hands over his ears while Billy was struggling back onto the front seat.

"Gawd amighty, Billy...you dumb shit! You asshole, Billy!" Myron opened his eyes and slowly turned to look in Billy's direction.

"You know damned well you're supposed to carry that gun with the safety on."

Billy was sitting upright, struggling with the riot gun, which was entangled with the microphone cord of the radio. Myron hauled off and backhanded him across the face, knocking him against the right side door.

"You stoopid bag of frog terds...you damn near kilt me with that gun. How many times I told you? You don' never carry a weapon like that inside a car with the safety off."

Myron yelled as loud as he could, drawing his hand back for another whack at Billy but he restrained himself. Billy winced but didn't duck. Men from the other cars were gathering around us.

"Hey, Myron. What the hell's goin on?"

"Hey, man. Did he try to escape?"

"Hey, let's hang 'em right here." Myron rolled the driver's window down and signaled quiet.

"Everythin's awright, boys. Billy, here, just got a little trigger-happy. Nothin to worry about. I told him he'd have to wait a little longer fore he blows a hole in this O'Keefe bastard. Now, get back in your vehicles and let's get on with this parade afore somebody figgers out what the hell we're cookin up."

He rolled the window back up and turned very slowly around, looked at Billy and then at me with a sinister grin.

"You're a right smart fella, O'Keefe. Too bad we don't have yah on our side. We could use a few good heads what with everythin gettin more complicated by the minute. But you done too much damage. I jest gotta keep you outta the way for a couple more hours and it'll be all done. So, jest sit there and shut up." He started the car and turned to look at Billy, "An the same goes for you, meat head." Billy winced again.

Now I knew how far I could push Myron and it wasn't far. He was a man on the edge and everyone around him knew it, yet they all seemed to give him a certain amount of loyalty that only a leader of great vision and outstanding qualities could command. Then again, maybe that loyalty had to do with the money. It's amazing what people are willing to die for. Take me for instance. Why the hell was I here? Was it the money? I could make a lot of money in other ways and never have to risk my neck doing it. No, it wasn't the money.

"So what is it, Mr. O'Keefe?" A little voice in the back of my head was asking? "Why are you here with these crazy people, heading for what is obviously your own demise? Is it idealism? Do you hate insurance fraud so badly that you'll do anything, even stick your neck deliberately into the hangman's noose, just to put a stop to it? All those great speeches about the state police and the F.B.I. investigating the death of Murry Berman? Was that all just hot air or do you really want to rid the world of all crime, filth, injustice, and fluorocarbons? Are you a masochist or are you just plain stupid? Ah ha! I've got it," says the little voice. "Your name is really Percival and this is your quest for the Holy Grail. You're ridding the world, as we know it, of all injustice."

"Try Robin Hood!" I said out loud.

"What? Whadya say back there?" Myron craned his neck around to look at me.

"Nothing really. Just thinking out loud...Say Myron. When's the payoff taking place?"

"Well, I guess there ain't no problem tellin you what's goin on. You ain't gonna do nothin to stop us from now on. Ole Frank Stillman, he said not to tell you nothin, but he don't count anyway, right Billy?" Billy winced, then nodded. "We do the dirty work and ole Frank jest pulls the strings. We're the ones what make it all happen. Ole Frank, he jest thinks up schemes, but me and the boys make 'em work. So, Frank, he takes the train into the city today, picks up the check and brings it out to the poor widder woman, Liddy Berman. He gets her signature and we go down to the East Island Bank and Trust where him and Rick Wallace are on the board. They play round with that computer and they break that check up into little bitsy pieces and everybody gets some of it."

"Only some people get more than others, right Myron?" I said.

"You got a big mouth, O'Keefe, but I got patience so it don't worry me none what you say. You ain't long for this world and neither is your girlfriend. Just in case you don't know it, Mista O'Keefe, your girl friend, Connie, is among the missin. We decided to let Rick Wallace have her, an after he finishes, there's a few more good ole boys gonna want a piece of that action. Do you hear me, O'Keefe. We got yer girlfriend. Ha, ha, ha, ha," cackle, cluck, cough, cough!

"Hey Myron, have you talked to Rick Wallace today?"

"Whadya mean? He's busy. He'll call me when he's ready to hand over the girl. That's what he said, right Billy? He said not to bother him, cause he'd be busy. Ha, ha, ha, ha," cough, cough.

So, they didn't know about Hank Gaines and the three kidnappers at Connie's apartment. If they learned that the state police were onto them, they might decide to bolt, and that could make it harder to prove their involvement in the whole scheme. Myron took the East Harbour turnoff and his caravan followed. We parked beside the police station and everyone gathered around, each one pointing a gun at me. This wasn't the time to make my break. My Caddy was parked near the back of the building. It didn't look like anyone had checked the trunk. It's always a pleasure dealing with amateurs.

"Alright, O'Keefe. Inside and don't try nothin. These boys'd love to blow yer ass to hell right now. You understand me, son?"

"Yes, master." I deliberately walked slowly, not letting anyone hurry me. The inside of the police station was old like the town hall. We entered a large room with chairs and benches made of oak. The hardwood floor needed refinishing. At the far end of the room the words "Cell Block" were stenciled crudely on a large steel door with bars. The dispatcher was to the right in a cage and to the left was a glassed in office and stairwell.

"Keep movin, O'Keefe! We got no time for sight seein." Two shotguns were pointed at my back and two more at my chest. I continued on slowly and deliberately, looking intently into the eyes of each man who held a gun on me. I learned that one from my C.O. in Vietnam.

"Stare your captors in the eye, not belligerently, just intently, like you're analyzing his brain cells. It'll make it harder for him to kill you, but easier for you. You'll memorize his face and hate him all the more."

A corridor ran down the middle of the cellblock, with three cells on the right and two on the left. Each cell had a small barred window up high above eye level, a cot, a washbasin, and a toilet. A single light bulb with a pull string hung from the ceiling. They put me in the middle cell on the right and locked the door with a large brass key. Like I said, amateurs.

"Hey Myron how about taking these handcuffs off? I can't hurt anyone in here."

"We'll leave them on yah. I ain't taken no chances."

"Myron!" I figured now was the time. "You're a useless, fat terd and I'm going to enjoy killing you." I stared him intently in the eyes, deliberately forcing myself to smile. His face turned pink, then red, then a dark purplish tinge began to rise up his fat neck and jowls. His hand, dangling at his side, began to shake, his eyes bulged, and his jaw quivered. Man on the edge. I was playing a very dangerous game.

"I ain't got time for this right now ... you hurt my men. When I get back we gonna decide how you'll pay for all you done." He was shaking all over with rage.

"At least your brother, Sammy, had the guts to stand up and shoot it out like a man, instead of hiding behind the skirts these other men."

"When I get back, O'Keefe, you'll be sorry you said that. I'll show yah what kinda man I am..." He turned and looked at everyone around him.

"All of you can go on home now. They's no reason for any of you to get involved any deeper in this thing. It's enough that you know it's done. Yah don't need to know how. Tomorrow's the payoff. You'll all get your share just like I promised and you know I never break a promise. Now, come on, move it out. I gotta meet Frank Stillman at the train."

Everyone moved to the outer office with some grumbling and the big steel door slammed shut. I could hear voices, car doors slamming and engines starting as cars drove away. It was nearly 6:00 PM and if all went as planned, Frank Stillman would have the claim check and be on his way back to East Harbour on the Long Island Railroad. Myron would meet the train and he and Frank would deliver the check to Lydia for her signature. They would do that much legally. Myron would be there to protect his interests and those of his local good ole boys who'd helped in the conspiracy. He had to make sure Frank and Lydia did as they were supposed to. No doubt, the East Island Bank and Trust Company would remain open after hours to insure the safe and immediate deposit of the endorsed check. My problem was very simple: remove the handcuffs, open the cell door, open the big steel cell block door, overpower the guards, get to Lydia Berman's, stop the payoff, and get out of town in one piece. I probably had about a half hour to do it. No problem!

Removing the handcuffs wasn't difficult. I moved my hands under my butt and stepped back over my hands. Why don't the guys in the movies do that instead of crawling around with their hands behind them, trying to untie knots or saw through chains they can't see? I pulled a piece of spring steel rod out of the sole of my shoe and used it to pic the locks on the handcuffs. They came open without any difficulty. The cell door presented another challenge. It was an old three-tumbler system. I got two of them the first try but the third wouldn't budge, so I took the other piece of spring steel rod from my left shoe, bent it 90 degrees and picked up the third tumbler. The lock made a ringing sound louder than I expected when it snapped open. Before I could step back from the bars, the cellblock door banged open and Billy came stalking down the corridor with his shotgun. I stood with my hands behind me, my head against the bars next to the door.

"Myron told me you'd try somethin. What the hell was that noise?" He pointed the shotgun at my chest.

"Billy, I gotta take a leak and I can't...you know...I can't."

"What can't you? What is it you can't?"

"You know...I can't get it out...could you...?"

"Myron said not to take off your handcuffs for anything. I ain't gonna take them off and that's that."

"Well... then...ahh, Billy, would you help me...you know..."

"What? What the hell are you talkin about?"

"Help me, damn it! Take it out for me so I can take a leak."

"You crazy man? I ain't touchin you. What the hell you think I am anyway? I don't do that stuff. No way."

"Okay, Okay. I don't blame you." I acted as if I was in real pain. "Can you just undo my belt for me? You know, just unbuckle my belt and I'll do the rest. I'll pull my own pants down. You don't even have to watch if you don't want to...or do you want to watch?"

"Watch what? What you talkin about?"

"You know ... watch me pull my pants down."

"My gawd! You a queer? Man, wait till I tell the other guys. They'll never stop laughin. I'll be damned. You a queer, by gawd.

"Hey, knock it off, Billy. I really gotta take a leak, bad. Can you help me out?"

"Okay, but no funny stuff. Step closer and I'll unbuckle your belt but don't pull your damned pants down until I've gone, you hear me?"

"Sure, I hear you." I stepped closer as he lowered the shotgun and started to reach for my belt buckle. He instinctively lowered his head to look at what he was doing and I gave him some extra help by grabbing his hair and pulling as hard as I could, banging his head against the bars, at the same time grabbing the shotgun away from him with the other hand. He was strong and quick, almost too quick, but I had the advantage and the element of surprise. I opened the cell door, pushed his head into it, and slammed the door on his skull, twice. He was out after the first time but it just felt good to do it twice. I dragged him into the cell, went to the steel cellblock door and opened it a crack. The dispatcher, a young fellow, was in the outer room. I stepped through the door quickly, leveling the shotgun at him through a space in the door of his cage.

"I don't really want to kill you, son, but I don't have much of a choice. Now put up your hands and open this door or I'll blow you in half!" I clicked the safety off just for emphasis.

"Don...Don't...Shoot! Please..." He stood up quickly and opened the door so fast I almost lost the riot gun.

"Where are the keys to the cells?" He pointed to the wall next to the radio. I stepped into the cage, picked them off the hook and motioned for him to come out after me.

"Into the cell block and take it real easy." He literally ran past me and into the cell with Billy. I closed the door and locked it, put the keys in my pocket and left, closing the big steel cellblock door behind me. I found my Colt .45 and extra clip in the dispatcher's desk, stuck it in my belt and went outside. I used a spare key from my wallet to open the Caddy, and drove slowly away to a date with six million dollars: Like I said: Amateurs!

Bay View Estates was east of town. I didn't want to attract attention so I drove slowly. Anyone could take a lucky shot at me. I passed the main harbor and continued down Bay Shore Drive, the ocean on my left and a high overgrown hedgerow on the right. After a half mile there was a sign that read Bay View Estates. The beach turned to rocks with a concrete revetment protecting the road from the pounding waves. Murry Berman paid big bucks for a view of the bay and got a high hedge, water in his cellar and no beach. I tried to recall the plot plan. Murry's house was in the middle of the development with a circular access road all the way around the outside.

I figured Frank and Myron would go straight to Lydia for the endorsement of the check and then to the bank. If I missed them here, I'd have to hustle to catch up. The houses all looked the same, long, low, ranch style construction, with few garages or driveways. The Cirelli brothers used little imagination in their development. At the fourth street on the left a police car was parked halfway down in front of a gray house with green trim. I drove past the house, turned around, parked about one house away and walked to Myron's police car. I placed a charge of C-4 with a detonator under the front-end frame next to the right wheel. I walked back to my car, took the .38 special I found in Rick Wallace's desk and put it in the right hand pocket of my sports jacket. I pressed the test button of the UHF activator. The green light winked on and I put it in my left pocket. I chambered a round in the Colt, lowered the hammer, and stuck it in my belt, no safety. I walked to a row of bushes separating the house from its neighbor, said a silent prayer to the god who oversees crazy people who become maverick insurance investigators, and waited.

Myron was first to come out of the house. He walked straight to his car without looking right or left, got in and started it up. Next came Frank Stillman, followed by a woman, Liddy Berman no doubt, dressed in a form-fitting T-shirt and tight jeans. She was a suburban, yuppie, housewife in top condition with trim hips, thin ankles, muscular calves, a big bust and short, dark pageboy haircut, no glasses. She shooed the kids back inside, kicked the screen door shut and turned to Frank. She put her arms around his neck and kissed him full on the mouth while pressing her body hard against his. He responded by kissing her back and grabbing her ample ass in his hands while grinding his crotch into hers: so much for the grieving widow. Calvin Kinderhook was right. The kids in East Harbour get run over in the yuppie stampede for success.

I kept an eye on Myron. I'd already decided I would kill him if he tried anything. It would save the state a lot of time and money. I walked very slowly across the lawn and stood about thirty feet from the house beside a small Norwegian Spruce. I've always liked the Norwegian Spruce. It possesses a perfection and clarity of purpose like little else in our world: straight, full and clean, reflecting light off its branches with a variety of unique colors and textures. I waited, taking long, slow, deliberate, full breathes of clean air...a good day to die, an even better day to kill the enemy and win the war. Either way, it would end right here.

Frank and Liddy finished their mating dance and she went inside. He stepped lightly off the low cement front porch and started across the lawn to Myron's police car.

"Frank!" I moved quickly toward him from behind the tree.

"What? My God...O'Keefe! What the hell...Myron said..." He glanced at the police car.

"Myron's full of shit, Frank, just like you..." I came up and stepped squarely in front of him, blocking his path to the car.

"Everything go alright in there, Frank? Did the grieving widow sign the check like a good little girl?"

"This doesn't concern you, O'Keefe. Now, if you'll excuse me, I have an appointment..."

He tried to push me away. I grabbed his hand and twisted, heard the crack and felt his wrist bones breaking. He cried out and I heard the sound of a car door being opened behind me. I pulled Frank around, cupping my left arm around his neck in a chokehold. We were both facing the police car and I was using Frank as a human shield. Myron pointed his S&W .357 at us. It was a standard model with a four-inch barrel and a custom made walnut grip. Lots of cops have them but not many can hit anything outside the firing range. I was about to find out how good he really was.

"You bastard, O'Keefe! Let Frank go or I'll kill yah both."

"Please...Pl...Please, Bill," Frank pleaded. "He'll do it. I know him. He'll kill us both."

"Where's the check, Frank?"

"In my pocket...please, it can work better than you can imagine. There's millions out there just for the taking. You can help us."

"Sounds good to me, Frank, but Myron doesn't like me any more."

"I'll fix it, Bill...just let me go and I'll talk to him...Okay?"

Only, Frank never fixed anything. Myron started shooting and even as bad a shot as he was, he hit Frank three times. I felt all three bullets strike his body. I couldn't get the Colt out of my belt because of the way I was holding Frank and I knew that if I let him fall, I would become the target. I pulled out the little Chief's Special from my right jacket pocket and emptied it at Myron who was still behind his car. I aimed at the open side window. My aim wasn't that good between holding Frank, being shot at, and trying to fire an unfamiliar weapon from the hip around another man's body. I was lucky to hit anything. We were only about 25' apart but one of my shots got lucky, passed all the way through the two open car windows and hit Myron in his big gut. I heard him cry out as he danced around in a circle holding his belly. He climbed into the car and peeled out. My weapon was empty and he was out of sight around the corner before I could let Frank down to the ground.

Myron was gunning the engine of the police car and I judged he would soon make the turn out of the entrance of Bay View Estates and start along Bay Shore Drive. He'd be reaching for his radio, calling for help. I pulled the remote control detonator out of my left pocket, armed it by turning the switch to "ON", held it up in the air above my head, pressed the button, held it down and started to count just like the instructions said. On the count of three, I heard the explosion. I must have used more C-4 than I thought because the blast was loud, reverberating like rolling thunder, not muffled as I expected it would be. Then I realized the charges I'd planted behind the police station and at Rick Wallace's insurance agency had gone off also.

I bent down and looked at Frank. He was in a sitting position, leaning against my left leg, making strange little choking noises. I held him up and opened his jacket. He'd caught a slug in the right shoulder, one in his stomach and a third on the left side of his upper chest. The last one was the fatal shot. I checked his pockets. The envelope was in his left coat pocket with blood on it but the check was undamaged. I read the signature, all neat and proper, "Lydia Berman", the happy widow. I stuffed the check and the envelope into my jacket pocket, wiped my prints off the gun and put it in Frank's hand. Lydia Berman was standing on the front porch, her face white and devoid of all expression. I laid him down and stood up as she came running and threw herself on the body, hysterically sobbing and beating his chest.

"You'd better call for help," I said as I walked away.

No phone calls would reach the police station but it would give her something to do as I drove away. Cars were stopping to my left as I pulled out of the entrance to Bay View Estates so I turned right. As I drove along the twisting shoreline of the bay, I could see the police car upside down in the rock-strewn surf and plumes of smoke rising behind me in the center of town. There would be weeping and wailing in the homes and halls of East Harbour this very night.

The sun was low in the western sky, disappearing in a haze of smog over the city and the smoldering Jersey dumps beyond. All in all, it had been another one of those beautiful sunny summer days out here on the Island. The sort of day where you would love to just kick back and relax, take it easy and enjoy the beauty of it all.

Unfortunately, for the people of East Harbour, it was not that sort of day. As I drove out of town and headed back to my cottage in the dunes, I wondered what Murry Berman was thinking just before he died. ✤

CHAPTER NINETEEN

The loose ends always take longer than the actual investigation. I spent several days just repairing the damage to the cottage. Connie's car required a new window and my Caddy had some bullet holes that needed patching. Hank Gaines advised me to stay out of East Harbour for a while until he could sort things out. I was replacing broken glass in my guest room the day he came to visit and gave me the official version.

"Looks like Myron Gates and Frank Stillman had a difference of opinion in Lydia Berman's front yard. They shot it out and Frank wounded Myron, using a gun belonging to Rick Wallace. Myron killed Frank and in the process of fleeing the scene, lost control of his car and crashed into the water and drowned. There were some questions about the extra damage to Myron's car but no one seemed interested in looking into it. Lydia Berman is hysterical and can't remember much about what happened. Rick Wallace is charged with kidnapping, conspiracy to commit murder, and accessory charges. Roy Stillman, Frank's brother, admitted to murdering Alexander Bench, the architect, and implicated Mrs. Bench, Myron Gates and Frank Stillman. In return for limited immunity, Roy Stillman told us what happened to Mr. Norman, the man who disappeared three years ago. Seems they were running the same scam. Frank Stillman sold him a $200,000 life insurance policy and Myron was supposed to drown the man. Instead, Myron lost his temper, got into a fight and beat him up. Then he shot him. He couldn't produce an acceptable corpse, so he buried Norman with the help of Roy Stillman and a Billy Cirelli, the fellow you locked up in jail. We've recovered the body in an old potato field and charges are pending."

"What about the payoffs to the widows, Norman and Bench?"

"We can't prove that. Evidently, Frank Stillman came up with $20,000 for Mrs. Norman to keep her quiet. We're trying to trace the payment to the Bench widow but there doesn't seem to be any record. State Mutual can't find it and, frankly, they aren't being too cooperative."

"You might try East Island Bank and Trust on that one. Even if they wiped out the accounts, the Telex charges and amounts sent to numbered accounts would be on record. That's required by law and it's a small bank, not as good at covering its tracks like a big insurance company."

"Good point. We'll try that. The shooting of Harry Dondi seems to balance out against the attack on you by the four men in the black pickup truck. There were enough witnesses to back your story. The four men killed here at your cottage are covered by Connie Wilson's testimony. You're lucky as hell to have her on your side. Without her you'd be in a tight spot."

"Oh come on, Hank! That was a hit ordered by Myron Gates. Don't tell me no one else knows anything about it."

"Well yes, Roy Stillman has mentioned it but that's not too solid. We'll go back and nail it down. The State Attorney General is chomping at the bit to indict you for murder but I suspect that won't happen. I made my report to the governor, in person, and when he found out he'd been used by John Stanley to impede a murder investigation, he washed his hands of the whole thing and told me to handle it. When I got the Phong Pho message, I knew we'd been had and I didn't give any more information to the Governor. When this is over, O'Keefe, you're gonna have to tell me just how this whole thing happened."

"I'll be glad to, Hank, but there are still some things I'm not sure about. For instance, how did they kill Murry Berman; and how much did Murry know about the sewer project and the payoff to the SARTXE Corporation; and who the hell is SARTXE?"

"We confronted Sophie Gates on the spider web incident in the town hall. They used that artificial spray stuff that you see all over windows at Halloween. She denies it was anything but a joke. We checked Murry's car and found a nail jammed into the seat belt roller. There was a plastic spider in the bottom of a coffee cup under the front seat. We confirmed that with the girl at the donut place. She said she thought it was a joke so she left it in the cup. Berman got a raw deal and now there are more widows and orphans in East Harbour than in any one single small town in the state. They just got too greedy. Six million is enough to bring out the worst in anyone." Hank stood up, stretched and looked out the window at the sand dunes.

"You got a nice place here, Billy. I should have done like you and cut loose, but I've got too much time in now to just walk away. Another three years and I'm retired..." He turned to face me and hesitated for a moment.

"There's one more thing about the East Harbour situation. The damage to the firehouse, the police station and Frank Stillman's place. Well, there's talk of charging you with arson and terrorism and anything else they can think of. I pointed out that they can't prove it, and besides they were all involved in a conspiracy to commit fraud and murder but they're pretty riled up. Just thought I'd let you know."

"I appreciate it, Hank. I know I dumped a pretty big load on you with this one and I'm sorry, but it was too big for me to handle alone."

"I don't know about that, Billy. From the looks of the body count and the collateral damage to the town, I'd say you handled it pretty well. It was them that was outnumbered, not you."

"I look at it this way, Hank. If we could ask Mr. Norman, Alexander Bench, and Murry Berman their opinions about how much damage should be visited upon East Harbour, what would they say?"

"Yep! I see your point. That's a real good one. I'll lay it on the

Governor. I've got an appointment to see him tomorrow to report on this case. Only thing is, good buddy, some of us learned our lessons real well in Vietnam and then we came home and started over. You gotta understand that, friend. The war is over. Give it up."

"I keep trying. Honestly, I keep trying but then I see things happen that shouldn't and I'm right back there again."

"Try to contain yourself. It's always a pleasure working with you but I got six months of paperwork on my desk because of this case, so why don't you take a long vacation and let me get caught up?"

"I'll do my best, Hank," and I did.

Connie came to visit for a week and we went sailing. It was like living in a dream world. Everything we did was fun and I felt years younger. The best test of any relationship is to spend time together, and the ultimate test is to spend that time in the closely cramped quarters of a sailboat. Any man and woman who can get along on a sailboat for a week, deserve an award. We did it and enjoyed every minute of our time together. Connie went back to East Harbour after the week was over, leaving me time to think.

There were several of those loose ends still gnawing at the back of my brain. It wasn't like I felt compelled or anything. I didn't even feel the need to solve the mystery of Murry's death. It's just that...well...if they killed him, I owed it to myself as an investigator to find out how it was done. I could accept his death as an accident if that's really what it was, but if not, then as a professional I wanted to know how they did it. So, that's why I went back to East Harbour, that and the fact I had a very unprofessional desire to see Connie again. I knew I shouldn't go there so soon, but I went anyway.

In the center of town, the firehouse and police station were under construction. They had moved fast. A taller tower was mounted on the police station and a cyclone fence surrounded the back of the firehouse. It really wasn't high enough to keep out a hardcore terrorist like myself. I swung by Frank Stillman's house and found a wrecking crew tearing it down. Nobody even looked my way and I didn't stop. I called Connie from a pay phone at a small strip mall near the beach.

"I've been wondering when you'd call. Park out back. I'll leave the door open and be careful, Bill, there are still a lot of bad feelings around here. Also John Stanley has been calling for you."

"I'll be careful, Babe. Just keep the home fires burning and don't worry about Stanley." I did as she said and parked around the back of the hotel. It wouldn't do to run into any of the local population.

Connie was in a good mood and glad to see me. "Don't worry about Rick Wallace. We're foreclosing on the hotel so he won't be around. Sit down and have some chicken noodle soup. It's lunch time and I'm starving."

"Connie, there's something you should know. Chicken noodle soup is all right in an emergency but if we're to have a successful relationship, we have to eat some real food, like steak and potatoes, or meatloaf, or lobster, or anything, but not just chicken noodle soup."

"But Bill, darling, chicken noodle soup makes me horny. It's the only thing I like before and after I make love."

"Okay then! Yes! I'll have some chicken noodle soup right now."

We were getting pretty good at making love. When two people have been thrown together in the heat of a dangerous situation they don't have time to really know each other. Now we were in a different phase, sinking, as it were, into a sort of domestic bliss. This is the stage where you find out if you're really compatible. Where does she hang her stockings? Does he put the toilet seat down? Does she squeeze the toothpaste tube from the bottom or the top? Does he put the top back on the toothpaste? Does she make the bed? Does he throw his socks on the floor? Does she snore? Does he snore? Who gets the computer tonight? Why does he sleep with his gun? And so on, until the new lifestyle becomes defined and you settle on who does what, and what is all right, and why it isn't, and you find out if you really love him or her and is it all worth it? I was thinking in these terms and wondering if I should feel out Connie on how she was thinking when she popped the question.

"Well, O'Keefe. You took me sailing and we passed that test and now you've come to visit and I've fed you and bedded you. So, when do I get to meet your kids and all that stuff, assuming you still want me to?"

"I want you to meet the kids and we can probably do it anytime because it's summer."

She looked at me intently and said, "Don't worry. I squeeze the toothpaste from the bottom and I put the cap back on the tube. I don't snore and if you do I'll sleep on the couch and if you don't want to wash dishes, I'll do it and you can dry. How's that sound to you?"

"Sounds good. How'd you know I was thinking about that stuff?

"Well, that's where we are right now," she said. "Don't forget that I was married before. I know it isn't easy. I didn't go as far as you did with the kids and house, and I'd like to do that some day soon if you agree but don't worry. I know that's all in the distant future right now, so let's just take it easy, go one step at a time, and see if we can do it the right way for once."

"Sounds good to me, Lady. Well, I can say this. I'm glad my ex-wife never bought an insurance policy off Frank Stillman."

"If she had, she'd be collecting millions right now." Connie laughed. I liked her laugh. It made me happy.

"That's the incredible part. It's not unusual for people who are unhappy to divorce, but it's perverse to take out an insurance policy on your husband and then participate in a conspiracy to murder him," I said.

"It's more than that, it's crazy."

"What troubles me is that it might go beyond East Harbour. If this thing spreads, it could cause widespread pain and suffering, not to mention the possible bankruptcy of the insurance industry."

"So, are you saying you're still on the case, O'Keefe?"

"Well, ahh...I haven't really..."

"And, can I surmise that you are here in East Harbour to find out how and why Murry Berman was killed and who was behind it?"

"I'm truly sorry, Connie. I really didn't want it to seem like this."

"I guess I'll have to get used to your dual personality. I see that it goes with the man, so for now, I'll do whatever I must to live with it."

"I'm not a hard man to live with but I'm also not a 9-5 type either. I like to finish what I start and that includes you. I may not always do things in the right order, but I eventually get it done, and nobody gets lost in the shuffle."

"So, tell me. How did this coffee cup and spider thing connect with Murry Berman's death?" she asked.

"Murry was a true phobic. There aren't that many around but they are there in the work-a-day world struggling to survive. We've all been repulsed by spiders, lizards and rats. We all feel 'Yuk', you know, repulsed when we see them but a phobic experiences a much stronger reaction, which is physical, not just emotional. We say phobics are afraid of spiders but they are really terror-stricken by the sight of a spider. They have physical reactions similar to an anxiety attack, only much, much worse. There's dry mouth, numbness around the lips and face, constricted throat, reduced vision, and nausea. Remember, Murry frothed at the mouth. The heart accelerates, then recedes and the blood pressure falls. They can't breath and systems begin to shut down as the victim goes downhill. The body pumps adrenaline to meet the emergency and the victim goes into a state of shock and can die if not treated. So, you can imagine how Murry must have reacted when he took the cover off that cup to finish his morning coffee. Maybe, he wanted to dunk his donut in the coffee and he saw that plastic spider. How would you have felt? Yuk? No, much worse."

"My lord," said Connie. "It must have been horrible for him."

"Yes, it was, especially when he remembered who gave him the cup just before he left home."

"His faithful wife, Lydia. Oh, no! How awful!"

"Now we step into the spider's web: Lydia Berman, the Black Widow."

"You're crazy, O'Keefe! She'll never talk to you after what happened. She'll scratch your eyes out."

"Maybe, maybe not. We'll have to play it by ear." We went through the harbor and started out Bay View Drive. Connie might be right, but I wasn't entirely satisfied, and Liddy Berman was the final stop. I turned into Bay View Estates and tried not to think of the last time

I was there. I parked the car and we went to the door of the Berman homestead. It looked unchanged as I knocked.

"Hello, may I help you?" Liddy still wore her T-shirt and tight jeans but she'd changed. She looked wilted.

"I'm here about the distribution of the check, Mrs. Berman." The expression on her face changed from a blank to one of surprise.

"I've been wondering when I'd hear from someone." She opened the screen door and we went inside. The house was nicely furnished in Spanish modern with deep pile beige rugs and raised velvet wallpaper. We sat on a red velvet couch in the living room.

"So, what's going on, Mr. what's-your-name?" She was shaking all over but she wasn't timid. I wondered if black widows attacked when they felt threatened.

"I've been in contact with the head office and they aren't entirely satisfied with the way things progressed here in East Harbour. I think the one thing we are most concerned about is that there should be no loose ends and no way of tracing anything back to the principal parties involved in the events leading up to the death of your husband."

"Speak English, mister whatever-your-name is. I don't know whose side you're on. You look familiar, so who are you and what's going on?"

"I'm on your side, Liddy. Surely you don't think Frank Stillman was smart enough to mastermind this thing, himself? Look at what happened. He handled it like an amateur. After the Norman mess they should have gotten rid of Myron Gates and his thugs."

"I told Frank he was crazy to trust Myron but he wouldn't listen, so look at what happened."

"Yes, precisely, Liddy. So, now we have the problem of covering everyone's tracks. We must be certain that the state police, the insurance commissioner, the state attorney, and no one else can track this thing or discover how it was done. We don't want the company implicated in any way, and that means you and everyone else must remain clean. Do I make myself perfectly clear?"

"Yeh, I guess you do. So, whadya want from me?"

"The spider, Liddy. Where's the spider? It's a loose end and we don't want it found."

"The spider? How the hell should I know? It's gone. Nobody found it. Damn it, that wasn't supposed to be my responsibility. I did what I was supposed to. The rest was up to Myron."

"So, you put the spider in Murry's cup and the seat belt was done by Myron?"

"No! Frank did the damn seat belt."

"Did anyone remove the implement from the seat belt roller so it could be used again like a normal seat belt?"

"How should I know? It wasn't my job. I put the damn spider in the cup. The rest was Frank's baby...Okay?" She seemed to slide away from us for a moment.

"Okay, but we better find that car, disarm the seat belt, and find that spider. Those are very serious loose ends. Now, there's the insurance physical. Was it Roger or Frank Stillman who did the physical?"

"It was Frank. I told him he was stupid to do it. He wouldn't listen."

"Yes, very stupid. He should have found someone else who was a closer match. Good grief, the eyeglasses and the difference in weight and height between your husband and Frank Stillman were enough to ring the warning bells for those insurance investigators. You have no idea how difficult it's been to plug the leaks? We've corrected the company records and the doctor's files but now we have to check the underwriter's distribution to make certain nothing exists elsewhere."

"What about Rick Wallace? Did he keep any records?" She perked up.

"Good point, Liddy. We'll check that out."

"So, when the hell do I get my million bucks? I should get more now that Frank and Myron are out of it. I've got expenses, you know? This has been expensive."

"This may take some time. Surely, Murry must have had some coverage through his work and then what about mortgage insurance?"

"The creep had a $100,000 policy but no mortgage insurance.

Can you believe it? A lawyer, and he's not covered enough to pay my damn house off."

"I see, yes...well, Liddy, you should count your blessings."

"Like what?"

"There's the million dollar policy Frank Stillman wrote on you, payable to Murry in case of your death, or if he preceded you it was payable to your current husband or to the children in a trust to be administered by SARTXE."

"What?" She stood up suddenly. "What the hell are you talking about? There's no such thing. Frank never did any such thing. Prove it. Let me see it."

"We've destroyed the policy. No sense in letting that sort of thing turn up anywhere. Are you saying you know nothing about this policy or SARTXE?"

"No! I've never heard of this what'd you call it?"

"SARTXE. It's a financial company. Perhaps Frank had other plans for you. It would appear you were to be his next victim."

"My god! No! He said he loved me. We were going to be married and go away, travel, put the children in private schools..." She started to cry. "Travel around...the world. Oh my, Geeze...No! He didn't really love me. The bastard used me. How could he...he said he loved me."

I stood up, "Perhaps we should go. We'll show ourselves out."

"The money. When do I get the money? I did what you people wanted; now I want my money. When do I get it?"

"Soon, Liddy. I'll clear it with headquarters and get right back to you. There is one more question, however. The morning Murry was killed, when you gave him his coffee cup and kissed him goodbye, what did you say?"

"What the hell does it matter to you? I did just like every other morning. That's what Frank said to do. I kissed him goodbye and said I loved him. So what?" She raised her head in defiance. ❄

CHAPTER TWENTY

We left Liddy on the couch, blubbering like a baby and drove away in silence. I took the road toward Brookhaven.

"You never told her your name and she didn't ask who I was," Connie commented.

"She didn't care. She only wanted the money."

"Yes, and she believed you when you told her about the insurance policy that Frank Stillman supposedly wrote on her for a million dollars. Is there really such a policy?"

"Yes, it was part of the computer records I took from his office. He was going to make millions and that included murdering Lydia Berman."

"How awful. Bill, this is the dirtiest business I've ever seen. Murder for profit but worst of all, these people were murdering people they were supposed to love. It's horrible. I don't know how you can stand it?"

"Oh, it has its compensations."

"Like what?"

"Like stick with me and I'll show you."

"I don't suppose you would care to tell me where we are going?"

"There is someone I would like you to meet. Hope you don't mind." I drove for about ten miles, took the exit after Brookhaven and picked up the South Shore Road. I'd been here so many times the past year, it seemed like my second home. We came to the entrance marked by two great stone pillars and a sign, "South Shore Retirement Home."

"This is where Willie Monk is staying. I always come to visit him when I finish a case. I hope you don't mind."

"Not at all. I'm looking forward to it."

As we parked, I recognized another car in the lot. It belonged to my attorney, Saul Goldstein. They were in the solarium, overlooking the grounds. Saul was perched on a wicker settee, reading from a book. Willie looked the same. He just sat there blank, not moving.

"Saul, Willie, I'd like you to meet Connie Wilson." Saul stood up and shook her hand.

"I am very pleased to meet you, my dear. Needless to say, Bill's description of you falls far short of the actual truth. Here, please have a seat." He moved over and patted the seat next to him. I took a wicker chair next to Willie's wheelchair. I put my hand on Willie's and squeezed it. There was a slight but perceptible movement of his hand. I looked at Saul in surprise and he nodded.

"Yes, the doctors say there is some improvement. They don't know why, exactly, but the nurses have been reading the newspaper articles about East Harbour to him everyday. It's like a contest to see who can find the most news around here. You're a regular hero and they think Willie is some sort of government agent. By the way, John Stanley has been calling."

"Let him wait. How about the offer we made on this place? Did they accept it?"

"Yes. I can't believe it but you were right. What a buy. It's worth twice as much. They're hungry for cash and this operation is too far away from their other homes for the parent company to manage it. I have other news. Natalie's attorney called me this morning and accepted the terms of your offer. It's done. No more haggling. No more monthly payments."

"How about East Harbour? Calvin Kinderhook?"

"All done. He's a bit nervous about it but I assured him it was legal. The only thing I question is giving Lydia Berman anything."

"If Lydia loses her house, she'll have to move and that will hurt the children. I agree, she doesn't deserve it but her children have lost their father and they don't need any more trauma. Of course, living with Liddy is pain and suffering in itself. Besides, she'll be under the watchful eye of Calvin Kinderhook and the East Harbour Widows' and Orphans' Fund."

"Do I dare ask what's going on here?" Connie asked with a quiz-zical smile.

"Can we tell her everything?" Saul asked.

"Sure. After I left Frank Stillman in Lydia's front yard, I drove around for a while trying to get my head together. Then, I went to your office at Daylight Inn and used the computer terminal on Rick Wallace's desk to tap into the New York offices of State Mutual. I had the codes, the number of the claim and the check signed by Lydia Berman. Most people think a check is like cash, but it isn't. The check has to be signed, cashed, and returned to the originating financial institution, in this case the New York office of State Mutual. So, that's where the money was and I just short circuited the process, went directly to the source and transferred the money to a bank of my own choosing."

"But, I thought all the banks were closed after hours."

"The bankers in the Grand Cayman Islands never sleep. They do business all over the world. If you know the codes, you can do busi-ness with them anytime and I did."

"But...but isn't that illegal?"

"No, not really. Considering, this whole scheme centered on murder and fraud, the money was really up for grabs. If I returned it to the company, no one would benefit but the company's board of directors, who might be in on it anyway and that makes them the real criminals. I came up with a different, more creative solution. The people who participated in the scam certainly don't deserve to benefit but there are a lot of innocent people who will suffer, so I decided to divide the money. Saul has the final breakdown."

"Yes, here's how it looks," he opened his briefcase and removed a piece of paper, which he handed to Connie.

East Harbour Widows'	
and Orphans' Fund	$1,000,000
East Harbour Education Fund	1,000,000
Berman Children's Fund	1,000,000
Lydia Berman	100,000
South Shore Retirement Home	1,200,000
O'Keefe Children's Fund	600,000
Daniel Mattos	100,000
SARTXE	1,000,000
	$6,000,000

The Widows' and Orphans' Fund," said Saul," is to help the families who have been devastated by this scam. The Education Fund is to help young people from East Harbour attend college. The Berman Children's Fund is for Murry Berman's children to be kept in trust until age twenty-one. These will be administered by a committee composed of Calvin Kinderhook, the current superintendent of schools in East Harbour, and myself. Lydia Berman receives $100,000 via a payment on her mortgage with a lien from the Widows' and Orphans' Fund so she can't sell the house for her own benefit. We've purchased this retirement home for 1.2 million to be placed in a perpetual trust under the name of Willie Monk. Willie will have a home for the rest of his life. By the way Bill, the doctors say there are some rehabilitation treatments for Willie that could help him. Now, Bill's 10% goes into a trust fund for his children, one quarter of the proceeds of which shall be made available to Natalie, his ex-wife, until the children reach the age of 21, at which time it becomes theirs. Daniel Mattos is the son of the harbormaster in Block Island. Danny receives $100,000 for the purpose only, of attending the Maritime Academy. There's a million left over for a fund, which Bill insists will be called SARTXE, EXTRAS spelled backward. An administrative fund to cover future expenses for O'Keefe's Investigations. Frankly, I think it's some sort of sick joke but Bill says it's part of his future and of course, we do need operating capital if we're going to expand."

"It's like our own SARTXE fund to provide a basis for future operations and we may need it after what was uncovered in this case." A nurse came in with a portable phone in her hand.

"Is one of you gentlemen, Mr. O'Keefe?"

"Yes, I am."

"There's someone on the line for you." She handed me the phone. It was John Stanley.

"Bill, my friend. Where have you been keeping yourself? I've been looking all over the place for you."

"I've been spending your money, John."

"Ah, now, Bill, you shouldn't do that. You should give it back. You don't know what you've done. You hurt us pretty bad there in East Harbour and you should make it up to us or there might be real problems in the near future."

"Like what, John? Are you threatening me?"

"Well, I wouldn't call it a threat but if I were you, I'd be looking over my shoulder. You should've played along, Bill. There's more than enough for everyone."

"You mean SARTXE, right John? SARTXE is nothing more than an illegal kickback scheme. You've had it, John. Your days are numbered so give it up."

"You don't know what you're messing with, O'Keefe." He was yelling. "You're going to regret this, believe me. You'll never be able to sleep again. We'll get you."

"Hey, John. Do me a favor, will you?"

"Yes? What is it you want?"

"Next time you send someone for me, send a professional will you? I'm tired of dealing with all these amateurs." I hit the disconnect button.

Saul turned to Connie, "Well, what do you think, young lady? Do you want to be associated with a group of thieves and reprobates like us, or would you like to just return to your former safe and boring life?"

Connie stood up and moved over to Willie's wheelchair, sat down on the table next to him and put her hand on his.

"Hi, Willie. I'm Connie Wilson and these guys want me to join up with you. What do you think?"

She smiled that smile that I'd seen the first time we met and Willie smiled back. So help me, Willie sat there and smiled for the first time in a whole year.

The End